Morgan,
when life knocks
you down . . .

SouthernHeartbeats Vol. 1

STAND

2

xoxo

jennifer rebecca

Stand

Jennifer Rebecca

Editing: Vicki Pierce

Cover & Formatting Design: Alyssa Garcia at Uplifting Designs

For Sean,

Thank you for believing in me even when I don't.
And also, for making all of my dreams come true.

PROLOGUE

Cody

This is it. This is that moment that changes your life. The lynch pin for the life you know you are supposed to live. This moment, this one right here, is mine.

It's the fourth quarter of the biggest game of the year. The biggest game of my life. This is the Super Bowl. My team and I have busted our asses for the last year to be here and we are here. We are mother fucking New York, baby.

My parents and my girl are in the team box watching. My parents, they're proud. I busted my ass as a kid in a small town in Texas to get to the NFL. I'm going to give my ring to my dad, the best guy I know. My girl on the other hand, she's not proud. She gets off on being my fiancée. She's after a different ring and I'm going to give it to her in the off season.

So here I am running to the end zone, fourth quarter of the biggest game of my life. Timmy, our quarterback and a crazy mother fucker all around waits until the very last moment to pass the ball across the field to me.

I leap up into the air like a mother fucking gazelle. No, they're weak. Like a mother fucking mountain lion on the hunt for my prey. I arch back to grab the ball from the air and see all the flashes. This image. This picture of me is going to be on the front page of every paper in the morning.

My fingers just touch the ball when I'm hit from behind by a Mack truck, or at least that's what it feels like. When my body hits the ground, the ball is in my arms underneath me and the human truck hits me again. I will never forget the sickening crack we all heard before everything went black…

Lights. Lights are bright. And blurry. Where the fuck am I? I blink again, trying to clear my eyes, when I see an angel. From the light up above me comes the most gorgeous girl with bright blue eyes and big, light blonde curls bundled up like my Granny's yarn on top of her head. She smiles a toothpaste commercial smile at me.

"Welcome back." But that's all I hear. Because when I try to ask my angel if I'm dead, everything goes black again. And the last thought I have is what a dumb fucking question to ask an angel. Of course I'm fucking dead. And now, now, I'm also a moron.

When I wake up again, there's a constant beeping that is driving me slowly insane. It's like *Beep…Beep…Beep…* I open my eyes again and this time everything works. I see Kimmy and her perfectly styled red hair. Her gorgeous face marred by an ugly frown. She looks up and realizes I'm awake. I realize that I am in a hospital and that God awful beeping is my heart beating, so that's good, right?

"Oh, good. You're awake," Kimmy says coolly and I can't help but think her first words to me should have been something along the lines of *Yay!!! You're still alive!!!* But who am I to judge. "Look, your parents went to get a cup of coffee, so I'll make this quick."

"Okay," I say but it comes out garbled. Kimmy obviously needs no approval because she just keeps on keepin' on and with the words that come out of her mouth, I think I'd rather get hit by that guy from San Diego that's the size of an elephant again.

"Look, it's not you, it's me."

"What?" I ask.

"This just isn't working out for me anymore," she starts. "I signed on to be a football wife, not the caretaker to an invalid in Nowheresville, Texas," I hear a gasp from the door and see my mom and dad standing there with my angel, who is apparently a nurse. A really hot fucking nurse. But I can't care about that because this crazy person is ripping my heart out. And right in front of my mom, no less.

"I should probably go. I'm going off shift and Jackie will be your nurse if you need anything this evening." And with that my angel leaves me high and dry. I don't even know her name.

"You should probably go," I tell Kimmy. "And you should leave your engagement ring with my mom over there," Kimmy gasps.

"But I love this ring! You know how much I love it," she pleads.

"Funny, I thought you loved me," and with one last pleading look of her big brown eyes, she takes off my ring and stands. Kimmy walks over to my poor, sweet mom and places the ring in her up turned palm. Those eyes, they used to get me. I'd do anything to make her smile. And her puppy dog eyes got me every time. But never again. Brown, green, blue or hazel, I will never fall for another pair of lying eyes from any woman ever again.

ONE

Angellica

Six Months Later- NYC

"Call it," the ER doctor in the bay with us says, defeated. "Time of death 2307."

"No!" I scream. Furiously pumping my tired arms over a tiny little body in an effort to keep her heart pumping.

"It's over, Angie," Dr. Smith says to me. But I just shake my head. My arms still working overtime. I know, if I just keep going, I can save this kid. I can't lose this kid. "Clear the room," he says to the rest of the trauma team.

But I can't stop. It's like if I lose this one kid, I have lost them all. I see horrors of all kinds as a Pediatric Trauma nurse in one of the largest hospitals in New York. But this one, was different. This child was thrown from a vehicle his parents crashed after having one too many glasses of wine at dinner. This child could have been saved if they would have just taken the train. Or a cab. God knows there are tons of them here. I choke back a sob and a tear burns down my face.

"Angie, let go," Dr. Smith says from behind me, his hands on my shoulders.

Dr. Smith is such a nice guy. A little older than me, wife and kids. How he balances all the bad with the good I will never know. But he is right, I need to let go. So I nod my head and let go. I decide to try his brand of balance and look for my boyfriend, Dr. Joseph Alexander, to soothe my frayed edges. Technically, he's my boss here, but he keeps me going. He doesn't let me falter. Doesn't let me give up. And keeps me really fucking busy.

I tear off my gloves and mask, tossing them in the appropriate receptacle and with one last look at Dr. Smith, I walk out of the ER bay and down the hall. I stop at the nurse's station to see if I can find him.

"Have you seen, Dr. Alexander?" I ask Marie, our seasoned head nurse and mom to all. She looks me hard in the eyes before seeming to come to a decision of some kind. She nods once.

"I saw him go into the on call room," she tells me. I smile my thanks to her but she doesn't return it for one reason or another. Weird.

I make my way down the hall. This is right. I just need a hug from my partner in life, some reassurance, and everything will be ok. I round the corner and come up to the on call room where doctors and nurses can catch a break while on long shifts. I open the door and stop in my tracks.

"You have got to be fucking kidding me," I say. And fucking is definitely an appropriate choice of words because my boyfriend, Dr. Joseph Alexander, is plowing Nurse Erin from behind in a way that would make a Midwestern farm boy proud.

"Do you mind?" She whines. Neither of them are looking to see who is watching their liaison.

"Uhh, yeah, I fucking mind!" I shout, slamming the door open against the wall so it makes a sharp crack. Now, that, Joe notices.

"Oh, Angie, it's not what you think," he says to me. I tip my head to the side trying to understand the words that are coming from his mouth as he humps the slutty nurse.

"You want to try that again, when your dick isn't deep in the hospital slut," I snap. Erin growls. And that asshole is still moving his body in and out of hers. Granted it's slower than before, but he doesn't even have the nerve to stop after he's been caught.

"Actually, I'd kind of like to finish up here," he snaps back. Erin snickers. "And I've been meaning to catch up with you, but I think we should open our relationship up to other people. Would you like to join us?" Umm, say what?

How has my life gotten this crazy? How is it that I am at a juncture in my life where my exclusive boyfriend is asking me if I want to hop into a threesome with him and the bitch I just caught him cheating on me with? Yeah, buddy, I'll get right on that. Uhhh, no. Not just no, but hell no. And also, now looking in from the outside, I can see, Joe really does have kind of a small dick. And he is probably the worst boyfriend in the history of the world. So, I do what any self-respecting woman would do. I take my phone out of my pocket and slide the little camera icon up and snap a bunch of amazingly unattractive pictures of Erin and Joe and Joe's very tiny penis.

"Yeah, I don't think I'm going to be available," I say calmly. "And I quit."

"Now, just a minute, you can't quit," Joe tells me. "This hospital needs you. I need you. Are you going to quit me too?"

"Oh, you betcha, effective immediately," I smile. "You should have thought about that when you started this. You know, I had come to find you because I had a really tough case and I needed to talk with my boyfriend, but more importantly, my boss, and both were unavailable." I wave vaguely at their disgusting display. I distractedly start typing on the keyboard on my phone as I turn around and head to the nurses station. My shift is about over so I don't feel bad about cutting out early, they'll be fine.

"Oh, and Joe, you might want to get that lesion on your dick looked at. It's not looking so good," I toss over my shoulder as I reach the door. Erin let's out a little shriek and tries to pull away and they both fall off the cot onto the hard floor. I can't help but laugh.

I make my way over to the nurse's station and sit down at one of the computers. I start with a new document and attach a picture and a handy little caption about the world's largest dick having the smallest actual dick and to watch your backs because he's one whoopsies away from a sexual harassment lawsuit or Venereal Disease. Whichever comes first. And then I hit print times one hundred copies.

"You ok, hon?" Marie asks me.

"Oh, I'm just peachy," I say in a way she knows that I am not as I carry on with my super important, bridge burning task.

I pick up the stapler and make sure it's full, almost like checking the magazine on a gun. I am locked and loaded, baby. And maybe just a bit unhinged. I grab my stack of handy fly-ers and start stapling them up randomly all over the ER, the nurse's station, the halls, the elevator. I even taped a bunch to the on call room. The whole time, Marie is watching me with a smirk on her face.

"You should know, Marie, Joe and I are no longer together," I inform her.

"You don't say, doll?" She says in a way I know she sees all.

"Oh, and you should also know that I no longer work here. Effective immediately," I tell her honestly.

"I figured that out the minute you started typing up those pictures of your man's teeny weenie. And by man, I also mean your boss. I'm sure I should tell you as your supervisor to take those down, but seeing as how you no longer work here, I am no longer your supervisor and am no longer inclined to offer up such advice," she shrugs. "But as your friend, I will tell you that you were always better than him and deserve so much more. So, go down the street, get yourself a pie to go for you and Mable and enjoy your evening with your aunt. Tell her I said hello and that we can all rejoice that you're no longer seeing that Shit for Brains. Pardon my French." With that she give me a big hug, hands me my purse out of the bottom drawer of my desk, snatches my security badge off my hip and shoves me out into the world.

"Oh shit," I say when I stumble out into the cool spring air. "I have no job. Shit." So, I do what any self-respecting woman would do. I do as I was told and I go buy Mable and I a mile high chocolate satin pie and head home to the brownstone I share with my aunt.

It takes me two trains and a bus, plus the walk from the bus station to home. And by the time I make it to the door, the weight of the day is heavy on my shoulders. I pull my keys out of my bag, but before I can ever reach the lock, the door is thrown open and my Aunt Mable is standing there in all of her glory. And she is glorious. At only fifty years young she is short and curvy, but not in a heavy way, in a Bette Grable pinup girl way. Her blonde curls, like mine, are artfully pinned up on top of her head and her gorgeous face has just enough makeup on it to be tasteful. Wearing her signature retired style, she is in jeans and a white poplin blouse. She is beautiful, but her face is scowling.

"Well, should we chop his dick off and cram it down his throat or rip his heart out and eat it?" She growls.

"I take it Marie called you?" I ask blandly.

"You know she did." Mable says unrepentantly.

"One of the casualties of working in the hospital your favorite aunt used to rule with an iron fist." I smile, lean in, and kiss her cheek. "I brought pie." I hold up the bag.

"Yippee! Pie!" She claps. "And I'm your only aunt." She laughs.

"Well, you can still be my favorite." I wink at her. And already, I'm starting to feel better. Aunt Mable has always been there for me, since the day I was born to a mother who could care less for me, and then again when my mother married a string of rich husbands, and then divorced them. And then again when she died in a plane crash last year with her last husband on some romantic trip I didn't even know they were taking.

"Well, I'll just go get that bottle of scotch that idiot at the Winkler Studio sent me for the showing last month. I hear it pairs well with pie and betrayal." Did I mention my aunt is awesome? And as part of being awesome, she's also kind of a famous painter. I say kind of because she won't admit to it. She says she likes what she likes, and she'll keep doing it as long as she damn well pleases, and if people want to pay good money for it, which they do, who is she to argue with them.

Two hours later, Aunt Mable is draped over a chase lounge like Cleopatra, but the bottle of scotch dangling from her fingertips kind of ruins the image. About two seconds after Mable offered me a highball of scotch I burst into tears and told her the whole sordid tale. At that time, she sat me down and handed me a bottle of vodka. Then Mable cut the big pie in quarters, dumped one in a bowl and handed it to me.

Now, the pie is gone, so is most of the vodka and scotch, a third of a tube of chocolate cookie dough, and the widow maker pizza we ordered from Giuseppe's down the block. Also, now, I feel like I'm going to puke.

"I feel like as nurses, we should have known better and eaten a vegetable." I tell Mable.

"What are you talking about? The pie was dairy, the pizza had sauce and meat, and vodka is made from potatoes. You can't ever go wrong with potatoes." I just shrug because yeah, potatoes are delicious in all their forms. And I didn't really want vegetables anyways.

"So, what do I do now?" I ask. Hoping my sweet, yet crazy aunt holds the secrets to life.

"Tall Pines." She whispers.

"Huh?" I ask. I am way too full and too drunk to be deciphering her own secret code of crazy.

"Tall Pines." She says louder.

"As in Texas?" I ask. We went back to my mom and aunt's hometown to deliver my mom's ashes last year. Otherwise, it's not a place we would just go to hang out.

"Yes. Exactly. I was just talking to Gertie at the Cut 'N Curl and she said Nurse Sarah died, so the school nurse job is open. You should take it."

"I feel like we should be more concerned about the fact that someone died." I tell her. I feel the shock on my face and can't even begin to try and hide it.

"Oh, pish posh. She was one hundred and twenty if she was a day. She lived a full and loooong life. Now, let's move to Texas."

"I can't just move to Texas." I tell her.

"And why the hell not?" She whips back.

"Umm…" I start.

"You have no car," She counts on one finger and I can't help but agree there.

"Umm…" But still, I have to try.

"No house, this one is mine." Shit. She's got me there too. She lifts another finger.

"Umm..." I start again.

"No job." She ticked off on her next finger.

"But…" I rally.

"And definitely no man." Well, that was just harsh. True, but harsh. She ticks off another fucking finger.

"Ugh. Don't remind me." I tell her.

"You fell on your face, baby girl. It's time to brush yourself off and stand back up." She says wisely. I just groan. "So, let's do it!" She cheers.

"Fine!" I shout. "I'll apply tomorrow."

"Here's my iPad." She says with a wink. "You can do it right now." She smiles slyly at me.

And damn it all to hell if I could say no to that. She even had the School district website up on her browser. Sneaky old woman! So, again, I did as I was told and applied for a job that I was sure I would never hear back about. So with thoughts of making my beloved aunt happy and a belly full of junk food and booze, I drifted off to sleep without one single thought of Joseph and heartbreak.

Angellica

Things went downhill pretty quickly. The morning after Aunt Mable and I had our heartbreak feast, this morning to be exact, I was thrust into the hangover from all hangovers by my ringing cell phone. As it turns out, when I was really drunk, Aunt Mable convinced me to apply for a job as a school nurse in the sleepy little town of Tall Pines, Texas; bayou adjacent mind you. Upon wiping the drool from my mouth and the crust from my eyes, I answered my phone.

"Hello?" I asked.

"Yes, is this Miss Andrews?" A sweet old lady voice asked.

"Yes, this is she?" I answer.

"This is Mrs. Truesdal, I am the secretary of Tall Pines High School. I'm calling to offer you an interview for the school nurse position."

"What?" I barked confused.

"The school nurse position. We would very much like to meet you, Ms. Andrews. I have a spot open with the Principal and the Mayor at four o'clock this afternoon."

"Ma'am, I'm in New York. I am fairly sure I couldn't make it there in time. I am very sorry." And also concerned because I cannot remember applying for a job in a town I have been to once in my entire life.

"My understanding is that all the arrangements have already been made. We will see you at the school at four o'clock." And with that she hung up on me.

I look up, unsure of what just happened. Clearly, people in Texas are straight up crazy. There is no way I can make it to Texas by this afternoon. I don't even have plane tickets to Dallas and then another puddle jumper to a small airport in East Texas. From there, it's finding a ride to Tall Pines. When I raise my gaze, Aunt Mable is standing in the entry way to the kitchen looking at me with a guilty smirk on her face.

"What did you do?" I growl narrowing my gaze on my duplicitous aunt.

"Just helping you get to Texas, baby." She says with a syrupy sweet smile and a wink.

"And how, pray tell, did you accomplish that?" I question firmly.

"Well, the owner of the Winkler owns another gallery in Dallas. I might have promised him a showing of originals that I will paint while we're in Texas — Tall Pines inspired. So he offered his private plane. Which is really great news," She hurries on. "Because we don't have to fly to Dallas first, we can go direct to Lake Miller Field." I sigh. She arranged it all. And with that thought, I ran to the bathroom and tossed my cookies, vowing never to drink again. Oh, the lies we tell ourselves.

While in the bathroom, I decide to wash the rest of the drunk out of my hair and off my skin. I brush my teeth twice and head to my room to get dressed. Deciding on comfort, I throw on my favorite dark jeggings that are secretly super comfy, a white vee neck t-shirt, a mustard yellow boyfriend cardigan and black ballet flats. I top it off with a multi colored paisley infinity scarf. I bundle my wet curls on top of my head in a messy bun and put my glasses on my face.

Quickly, I throw a decent interview outfit in my carryon bag and basic makeup bag. I throw more clothes and shoes in a duffle bag hoping against hope I didn't forget anything. I head to the kitchen to pour a pot of coffee in my face but I must have stood up too fast because all of a sudden I feel clammy and dizzy.

"Here, try this." Aunt Mable says as she hands me a glass with questionable contents. I raise a brow in question, but she merely shrugs and says, "Hair of the dog. You might want to just shoot it." She says showing me every bit of the formidable ER nurse she was. I like to think I get that from her.

It looks like a bloody Mary so I figure it can't be that bad. And let me tell you, I figured wrong. It was bloody Mary mix for sure, and it also had some vodka in it, but that was where the fun stopped because choking back the three raw eggs that bobbed around in it was tough stuff. I slammed the glass on the counter with a shudder and wiped my mouth with the back of my hand.

"Here, now chug this." The "this" in question is a bottle of pedialyte. At this point, I will do anything to feel better and get the taste out of my mouth of that foul bloody Mary. When I set the bottle down, I feel better. Like livable better. I can't believe I'm going to a job interview hungover. I'm moderately embarrassed for the state I seem to be finding myself in.

"Ok. I'm ready." I say as we make our way out of the brownstone, lugging our bags into the back of a cab, and make our way to JFK. As we drive over the bridge, I thought, what if I never came back to New York, would anyone miss me? And then I thought, I don't much care. Here's to my next adventure.

We don't go through the ticketing counter and security. Aunt Mable has the cabbie drive us through a back gate where our names are on a special list with security. He drives us all the way to the small hangars in the back where a small, sleek looking killer is waiting for us all shined up and freshly fueled.

A set of stairs folds down from the door, a smartly dressed man comes down and takes our suitcases from where the cabbie is unloading them from the trunk, and carried them up and into the airplane. I stare in awe at the plane, I have never traveled like this before.

"Well, are you coming or what?" Mable stares at me from halfway up the little stairs. I scurry out of the cab, throw my cute little coach purse over my shoulder, and grab my carryon with all my rations in it.

I climb the sleek chrome steps and am getting a little excited for this trip. When I walk through the door, there is the most gorgeous brunette smiling at me, telling me I can sit anywhere I want and that the bathroom was in the back.

I quickly stow my bag in the compartment and break out my iPad, thinking I'll relax with either a movie or a fun book. Maybe a romance with a hot baseball player or a sexy fireman. I take my seat next to Aunt Mable and buckle up.

I'm surprised to hear an attractive woman's husky voice over the intercom tell us that she is the Captain and that we should be taking off shortly. Girl power, I dig it. And it was possibly the smoothest flight ever. She taxied down the runway like a seasoned pro, takeoff was so easy, I was sure I was going to be sick since I was still a little hungover, but I never felt a thing. I look over at Aunt Mable, my eyes wide in surprise and she just smiles and winks at me.

I'm deep in my book about a handsome MLB player who is looking to end his wild ways and settle down with the girl next door, when the flight attendant places her hand on my shoulder.

"Would you like something to drink, Miss? I have juice, soft drinks, coffee, and a variety of adult beverages," she tells me. My stomach turns at the thought of more alcohol. I look over at Aunt Mable and she's daintily sipping a glass of champagne while she flips through some magazine like she does not have one care in the world.

"Maybe coffee. Black," I tell her. She quietly pours me a mug. Like a real mug. And I hold the warmth in my hands. Talk about snazzy. This plane pulled out all the stops. And for the first time I'm wondering exactly what the intentions of this gallery owner are with my sweet aunt.

My head is starting to pound, so I put my iPad away and shoot the second half of my cup of coffee. I lean my head against the cool glass of the window next to me until I feel slightly better.

I decide now is the time to try and make myself look half-way human. I unbuckle my seat belt and grab my bag from the cabinet and head towards the back of the plane. When I walk in the bathroom, I am dumbfounded. This is a real freaking bathroom. Like better than my bathroom back home. Whoa.

I quickly shut the door and set my bag on a stretch of granite countertop. I unzip my bag and retrieve my makeup kit. All it takes is one quick look in the mirror to know I look like hammered horse shit. Today, I will be pulling out the stops so they don't think I'm an escaped mental patient instead of a highly sought after registered nurse.

I lay out my makeup in order of operations. Hey, I have a logistical mind. First to bat is the shimmery concealer because those are some big steamer trunks under my eyes. Then I add a little tinted moisturizer to even out my complexion, which is still looking a little gray. How Aunt Mable is fine I will never know. She's a machine. And looks amazing doing it! Next up some powder and a sweet peach blush. I round it out with a shimmery nude eyeshadow and black mascara. It's not great, but it will have to do.

I toss all the makeup back in my bag as I go. I grab my brush, bobby pins and some hair spray next and make my bun look school marm professional on top of my head. I have a black suit of skinny slacks and a tailored blazer with a little kick out on the back. I match that with a white silk button down, stockings, and black pumps. I'm feeling pretty fantastic until I walk back out into the cabin.

"Jesus Christ, who died?!" Aunt Mable shouts and I wince when my brain seizes from the trauma of the shrill noise.

"No one. I was just getting ready for my interview. You know, so I look good?" I shrug.

"This is not New York, child. Go back in there and put on the clothes you already had on," She tells me sweetly.

"Are you sure?" I ask. When she just nods I look to the perfectly put together flight attendant and she also smiles sweetly at me and nods yes. So back to the bathroom I go.

I quickly take off my suit and throw my jeggings and t-shit back on. The pumps and hose I am not going to miss! My cardigan is so soft and comfy and my scarf ties it all together in a way that would make Pinterest proud. I add my favorite silver watch and the small diamond studs that Mable gave to me when I graduated college. They have brought me luck so far, and today I could totally use them.

As soon as I am redressed, I immediately feel more at ease. Mable knows me too well. I repack my bag and stow it in the compartment. Once I make my way back to my seat, I continue reading my hot baseball player book. Will he get the girl? Stay tuned. Before I know it, we are landing in Miller, Texas. Ready to catch some form of transportation to Tall Pines. Hopefully, the bus has a heater since it's still pretty chilly for spring.

When we exit the plane there is a big black suburban with a very handsome blond man sporting some pretty decent muscles holding up a typed sign that says "Ms. Andrews and Ms. Andrews" on it. In comic sans font. I snicker. Nice. Very professional. What is he? Twelve. Our friends from the flight unload our bags from the plane and help load them into the back of the suburban.

"Hi, I'm Sam. The OL Coordinator for the football team. You must be Angellica?" He asks moving to shake my hand. "And you must be the infamous Ms. Mable. You're legend around these parts," he says in the most charming way.

"Thank you for coming to get us, I really appreciate it," I tell him.

"It was nothing. Plus, my mother in law would have my hide if she found out I didn't show Ms. Mable the hospitality she deserves," damn, he's married. What the fuck is wrong with me. I just dumped my cheating ass boyfriend yesterday. And I'm here for a freaking job interview. Jesus, I am a psychotic mess. Mable clears her throat and gives me the side eye, clearly telling me that my silence is weird.

"Well, we appreciate it anyways, don't we, Aunt Mable?"

"Of course, dear. How is Sheila anyways?" She inquires.

"Happy as a clam since Sarah and Harper were born. Those are Aliza's and my girls. And we moved back here when I got out of the service."

"Of course. One day, my Angie will stop dating giant sacks of crap and will give me the great nieces and nephews that I deserve," she lets out a great put upon sigh. "Until then, I will have to come by and see yours." Aunt Mable is really laying it on thick over here and the more she talks, the thicker her accent comes back. It's a sight to see.

Before we know it, we are pulling into town and I feel my stomach muscles clench. I try and covertly wipe my sweaty palms on the thighs of my jeans but a subtle movement catches my eye and I see Sam's gaze is on my movements in the rear view mirror. His eyes crinkle in the corners so clearly he thinks I'm amusing.

"Right this way," Sam says and we all climb out of the suburban in the high school parking lot. He leads us into the building and just through the main doors speaks to a woman at the front desk.

"Is this our nurse?" The voice from the phone call this morning asks.

"Yes, Ma'am," Sam drawls.

"Right on time. They're ready for you in the Principal's office," she tells me.

"Come on, child, right through here," Mable says, dragging me along. I'm so nervous about the interview and so distracted by Mable. I can't say I've had her walk me into an interview in I don't know how many years, or like ever. But I swear I heard Sam and the school secretary continue to speak in hushed tones.

"She's pretty. He won't know what hit him," she says.

"Either one," Sam finishes as the Principal's office door snicks closed behind me.

THREE

Angellica

"Quit your struggling, child, and get in here!" Aunt Mable growls low in hushed tones as she drags me by my elbow into the Principal's office. I can't help but feel as if we've lived this scenario before. Mainly because we have. This Deja-vu moment is brought to you by the memories of Jimmy Fitzpatrick and me smoking and making out in the back of his 1988 Buick Le Sabre during lunch hour. In all fairness, it was a Le Sabre. Jimmy, however, turned out to be nothing to write home about. But really, what sixteen year old is. Poor kid kissed like a Saint Bernard, but I was fifteen, how was I supposed to know any better?

"I'm coming, old woman," I growl back in equally hushed tones. The snippets of conversation I had caught out in the front office have shot my carefully put together calm composure all to shit. "Quit man-handling me!"

Mable and I all but barrel roll into the principal's office in a tumble weed of legs, elbows, and four letter words befitting a sailor. I immediately stand and reach a hand out to help Aunt Mable up. She takes my hand and stands with the grace of a ballet dancer, not one fucking hair out of place. Seriously, how the fuck does she do it? I shake my head and brush some lint from the floor off of my jeans.

"Jesus Fucking Christ," I mutter running a hand down my face and look up into the laughing eyes of a man probably in his fifties, like Mable.

He has warm, sandy brown hair with touches of gray at his temples, bright hazel eyes, and laugh lines in the corners. His shoulders are broad and muscular as well as his arms and torso that ends, from what I can see, in a tapered waist below his desk. The Principal has a banging body for an older dude. Aunt Mable should hook it up.

"Hello, Ms. Andrews, I'm Principal Reynolds," the man stands and shakes my hand over his desk. He's got nice legs too, but I notice a wedding ring. Too bad. "Hello, Mable. Good to see you," he smiles at her. I turn and wink at her as she bats her eyelashes at the Principal when I hear an unmistakably feral growl come from behind me.

"Ah, Mayor Hart, I didn't realize you would be here," Aunt Mable says coolly. You can't mistake the rudeness in her voice. Principal Reynolds chuckles.

"Mable," I whisper. "Don't be rude."

"Of course I would be here. This town is my house. I make sure we keep the riffraff out," he says darkly and I turn around to come face to face with a tall, lean man with a hard face and cold as ice, blue eyes. Familiar eyes. But I can't figure out why. Or why he hates me. I'm pretty sure they called me, right? Or was that a drunk hallucination. It was vodka, not magic mushrooms, right?

"Well, I never!" Mable remarks. "I have no idea what you're talking about."

"You know exactly who I'm talking about," the Mayor barks.

"Maybe we should just go," Mable says. "I'm sorry to have wasted your time, Jim. Not nice seeing you again, asshole," she barks at the Mayor.

"Now, just see here!" He bellows.

"What about my interview?" The Principal hollers. "I still need a nurse."

"And you would have one if Mable wasn't being her usual self."

Whooowhooop! I whistle with my fingers in my mouth like I do at Yankees games. "If we could all just put our dicks away for a minute we can get this settled." I go one by one down the list of people in this office. "Mable, hang tight for a minute. Can you do that?"

"Yes," she says through clenched teeth, enunciating the sss like a snake.

"Ok. If I get the job you be nice. If not, we go out in a blaze of glory and tell these two what a bag of dicks they are. Although, I would like to add to the record that Principal Reynolds seems like a nice guy," she smiles one of her smiles that means trouble is coming and then winks. Mable is hell on wheels.

"Mayor," I turn to look him in the eye after Aunt Mable is settled. "With all due respect, what the fuck is your problem? I don't even know you. You guys didn't have to call me back, you could have just quietly passed on my resume. With that said, I am the best pediatric trauma nurse you will ever fucking find. You'd be lucky to have me as a school nurse here." When he just nods his head indicating I should continue, I do just that.

"Principal Reynolds," I start.

"Call me Jim," he smiles, his eyes twinkling with glee and mischief. That's a good start right?

"Jim, can I still interview for the job?" I ask softly.

"God, yes," he says and I jump in surprise. "Let's just ignore those two old birds." And just like that I smile the first real smile I've had in days, maybe months, as I take my seat in front of his desk.

"So, as you said, your resume is impressive," Principal Reynolds tells me something I already know.

"Thank you," I say because it seems the polite thing to do.

"Taught her everything she knows," Mable shares. And she is not wrong. She did teach me everything she knew before she retired to become a famous painter.

"So, at your last hospital, you recently quit," he starts and my back straightens.

"Yes," I say vaguely.

"On your application, when prompted why you left your last position you said, and I quote, 'Because I motherfucking can and that slut bag can have that pompous, limp dicked little weasel.' Care to elaborate?" He asks me with a twinkle in his eye. I hear Mable choke on a laugh she's trying to hold back.

"Awe hell," I say under my breath. To the Principal, I say, "No, sir. I think that is pretty self-explanatory and all," I look at the ground.

"Hey, we like honesty around here," he chuckles. "And glad to see any woman who won't take any shit. You'll need it around here."

"What do you mean by that?" I tilt my head to the side in question.

"Just that some of the football players in these parts can be pretty rough and tumble. They hurt themselves and they'll need someone who can be firm with them," I nod. It makes sense. Kids that driven, that cocky can be a real pain in the ass when they're in pain. "But also show them that they still matter, even if they can't play anymore," he says softly. I just nod.

"Makes sense," I reply.

"Now, we called on your references," I cringe. Joseph was my boss and my lover until last night. That's probably not going to be great. "A Dr. Alexander told us you were the 'worst nurse in the history of nurses and that we should hire, literally anyone but you.' I took this to mean he is the 'limp dicked little weasel' in question," I sigh and just nod my head.

"In the name of full disclosure, Dr. Alexander and I were involved until recently," I say. Aunt Mable just snickers. The old bat.

"I'll say," she laughs. I growl and give her the side eye trying to impress upon her that we should maintain some decorum.

"We took exception to this, especially considering the head nurse at the hospital said you were the best she's seen since herself and that you had saved countless kids, including mine. And also, that Dr. Alexander is a douche canoe," the Principal's eyes glitter with amusement. I just sigh. Again.

"Jesus," I say, swiping a hand over my face. Never catching the meaning of his words. I'm so screwed. Time to kiss this job goodbye. I can't believe I flew all the way down here, hungover to boot, just to be told I'm a total failure.

"That's my girl," Mable cheers.

"I think we can all agree, that you would be a great asset to the Tall Pines Independent School District," Principal Reynolds tells me with a kind smile. Umm, say what?

"What?" I ask, shocked.

"You're hired, Angellica," he says, smiling warmly at me.

"Angie," I tell him, absent mindedly.

"You're hired, Angie."

Not one to look a gift horse in the mouth, I said a quick thanks, signed every single contract, non-disclosure, and magazine order form they put in front of me before grabbing Aunt Mable the way she grabbed me when we entered the office and beat feet out of there.

"Huh..." We both said, shaking our heads.

It wasn't until we were standing in the parking lot of the high school, that we both realized our luggage was in Sam's Suburban and we had no car. Aunt Mable, never one to ask a man for help, muttered a quick, "Fuck it," before she started marching down the sidewalk. Like the smart girl I am, I followed.

Two blocks later, we were seated in the most amazing diner ever. If I ate every meal here for the rest of my life, one, that life would be short due to clogged arteries and high cholesterol, two, I would weigh four hundred pounds, and three, I would die happy. Mable ordered a hot roast beef sandwich with au jus, steak fries, and a large malt. Her metabolism should be studied by scientists. I ordered the hot opened face turkey sandwich that consisted of sourdough bread, stuffing, which the waitress informed me in the south is dressing if it isn't actually stuffed in something, thick slices of roast turkey, gravy, and the cranberry sauce on top of the pile, steak fries and a coke. It's like thanksgiving in my mouth.

I think I've died and gone to heaven. Mable and I are both quiet while we eat. The women in our family are pretty serious about food. Our bodies need it to be successful in life, but we also enjoy it and don't have any shame in that. When the check was delivered by an adorable brunette named Katy, Mable snatched it up and paid leaving sweet Katy a healthy tip. We grabbed our purses and made our way out the door into the warm Texas sunshine.

"That was quite a tip you left her," I comment off handedly.

"That's Marsha's girl, Kathryn. Her fiancée was killed in Iraq when she was only eighteen. Hasn't dated since. Lives her life like a lonely old widow, the poor thing." I immediately regret my thoughts about her tip and vow to do the same every time I eat there too. My Aunt Mable may be a pistol, but her heart is huge too.

We are walking aimlessly around the main part of town when we pass an adorable blue craftsman home with a large, beautifully tended yard, and a white picket fence. You could also see a gorgeous all glass solarium on the side that would make the best studio for a famous artist. The truly exciting part was when we noticed the big for sale sign in the front yard. Aunt Mable whipped her cellphone out of her purse and unlocked it, typing like mad, I'm watching her in a trance until her next words, not directed to me, pull me out.

"I'll take it," she says firmly. "My accountant will have the funds wired to you shortly. Thank you," before she signs off. Followed by her typing more things in a crazy fashion. Must be nice to be an eccentric artist.

"Harold…Yes, it's Mable….I just bought a house in Texas… Send money to this address," she rattled off the account. "Yes, now…I'm picking up the keys in an hour…You too…bye Harold." Damn, she works quick. Must be good to be a famous artist.

Mable makes a quick about face and starts heading back towards the diner. Just past it sits a local furniture store. Mable marches in like a force to be reckoned with.

"Can I help you, ma'am?" A young woman asks.

"Oh, we're just loo…" but I get cut off by General Mable.

"Yes, I want this sofa, that dining set, that bedroom set, this one over here too, that kitchen table, the china hutch that matches, these end tables, and this sofa over here," she finishes triumphantly. The saleswoman and I are both a little shell shocked.

"Mable?" I ask hesitantly.

"What? We need furniture and it needs to fit the house. The New York stuff is too stuffy, it's not fun," she shrugs. Well, who can argue with that? She's right too. That sweet blue house needs comfy furniture you're not afraid to live with.

"Okay," I say, because what else can you do?

"Now, go pick out a bedroom set for yourself. Chop chop!" Aunt Mable claps and then shoves me in the direction of a bunch of bedroom suites set up in the back of the store.

"Okay. Okay!" I shout as I run to pick out a beautiful white iron bed with an interwoven headboard, a large white dresser and matching night stands, and a mirror.

"I need all of these things and new mattresses and pillows, the best only, sent to this address in two hours," Mable tells the girl handing over a black credit card. Damn, it must be good to be a gangster. "Let's go! We have keys to pick up," she shouts.

We retrace our path back down the main street to a small real-estate office where Aunt Mable signs a few more papers but her accountant slash man Friday, did most of it for her at an alarming rate before we're handed sets of keys.

We again, retrace our steps back to the little blue craftsman with the gorgeous yard just in time to receive our household of furniture. Once again, Aunt Mable whipped out her cellphone and a short time later, we were enjoying pizza and lemonade on our new round, antique white kitchen table with ornate legs, matching chairs and china hutch. Who needs a suitcase when tonight I'm sleeping in a new bed and in a few days' time, I will start a new job. Mable was right, this new adventure is off to a great start.

FOUR

Cody

Thank, fuck. I think as I walk through the door of Our Father's Flag, the local watering hole that is owned by my buddy, Holt's family, for only about a million generations. It's a mix of dive bar and military memorabilia. It has been a rough damn day surrounded by crazy teenagers. I swear, I won't survive a year of teaching those little fuckers health class, sex ed, and driver's ed. My dad is clearly out to kill me.

Holt is just the most recent generation in all of the Stone's to serve their country, then come home to run this bar. Holt never wanted to run it, it was always supposed to be his twin brother Will, but he was killed overseas while I was away in New York, playing ball.

Holt came home and ran for Sheriff. Just like Sam came home a couple of years ago and became the Offensive Line Co-ordinator for our high school football team. I crapped out of the NFL in the fourth quarter of the Super Bowl and came back here to be the head football coach, you know, after re-learning how to walk. But lather, rinse, repeat, we all came home. One way or another.

I make my way to the darker, back corner of the bar and sit down in the very last booth, my back facing the door, and take a deep breath, my shoulders sagging in relief. I know what you're thinking, it's weird to sit down by yourself with your back facing away from the room, but I'm meeting Sam and Holt here, and those two can be cagey mother fuckers these days, so it's my little manly part to help ease whatever it is in their minds that has frayed edges.

Holt walks in and plops down on the bench across from me. Katy walks over and hands us each a beer she just poured. I smile at her as she winks at me. Holt just scowls as she walks away.

"What the actual fuck?" He growls. And I'll be damned if it doesn't catch me off guard. I might be a badass on the field, but I'm pretty sure Holt could kill me sixteen different ways with a pair of eyebrow tweezers.

"Umm, what?" I ask and I hate how shaky my voice sounds. Shit. I'm such a little girl.

"Is there something going on between you and Katy?" He asks straight out and I am dumbfounded as to why he would think that.

"Uhh, no," I tell him. "Why would you even think that?"

"Because she winked at you," he again says straight out. I like that about Holt, he never beats around the bush. That thought sends my immature mind directly into the gutter, and it's all I can do not to snicker, because no doubt Holt would take it the wrong way and punch me in the face. And I happen to like my face.

"Dude, she winks at everyone," I tell him. Holt might be losing it a bit. I look at him a little closer and he holds my stare, I'll give him that, something is going on with him, I'm just not sure what. But I'll figure it out. That much I'm sure of.

"Humphh," He concedes.

"Seriously. You know I am never getting involved again just to get burned again," he looks at me. Like really looks at me until he nods once. I swear if he looked at me a second or two longer, I would have crapped my pants. I'm man enough to admit that.

"Hey guys, what's up?" Sam asks as he slides into the booth next to Holt with an easy smile.

"Holt's lost his damn mind," I tell him. And he just chuckles.

"Is it over the new nurse?" Sam asks.

"What nurse?" I ask. I've been so busy with Spring Tryouts that I can't even remember my own name some days.

"The school nurse? Come on man, I know you've seen her," Sam asks, holding his hands out from his chest. Almost like he's holding a pair of imaginary cantaloupes.

"Why would I? She's probably some old blue hair, right?" I ask. Holt and Sam share a look before throwing their heads back, laughing. I think about their reaction to my question before it dawns on me. "She's a babe? Really?" I ask because I can't help it.

"You interested?" Sam asks me.

"Don't be stupid," I shoot him a withering look.

"So you wouldn't mind if someone else was interested?" Sam asks and this gets my Spidey senses tingling.

"You're not thinking of stepping out on Aliza are you?" I ask starting to get pissed. I see Holt stiffen next to Sam but wisely doesn't say anything.

"Of, course not, you moron. She is it for me. I meant Holt, you douche," he tossed a handful of bar nuts at me.

"Jesus, you scared me," I tell him.

"But still, you don't even want a look before someone else moves in? I mean it's kind of poetic, football coach and hot school nurse. Oh, God, do you think she has a nurse's uniform?" Sam asks, egging me on. He's been telling me for months to get back on the horse, but I just can't bring myself to do it.

"Nope. Not dating. Ever again, man. You know that," I tell him, eating one of the peanuts I pull out of the collar of my school polo shirt.

"So, Holt, can go after her?" He asks, sharing another mysterious look with Holt.

"Sure, man. Go get 'em, Tiger," I say and laugh.

"Cool, then don't turn around now" he tells me on a laugh. And it's like a god damned car crash, you can't not look. So, what do I do? I casually look over my shoulder and stop in my tracks. All the air in my lungs whooshes out because at the door to Father's is Angel. My. Fucking. Angel.

My fucking Angel from that hospital in New York. I would recognize all that blonde hair and big blue eyes anywhere. Not to mention full, dark pink lips that you know would be good for kissing and....other things. And, hello, she has been hiding a dynamite body under those awful scrubs. I hope she burns every last pair. She looks like one of those pinup girls from the old movies my mom likes to watch. And looking at her in tight jeans and a slinky pink tank top, I can't help but agree. Shit, I'm hard. Like the steel rod in my spine, hard. That's totally not awkward or anything since I'm sitting in a bar with my two best buddies. Ugh. I run a hand down my face and think of baseball. Nope, still hard. Shit.

Did she come here for me? I can't help but like that feeling. Holt puts his hand up to wave her over and she starts in our direction. My palms are sweaty and I'm a little nervous. I never thought I would see her again. Not that I didn't think of looking her up at that hospital she worked at every night when I had my dick in my own hand, but part of me didn't want her to remember me like the sad, broken man I was. I figured it would be better to leave her in my fantasies.

"Mind switching seats with me, man?" Holt asks. When pigs fucking fly, asshole.

"Over my dead body," I growl. "She's mine. My angel." I want to beat my fists against my chest. And those two morons just laugh.

"Hey, guys," she says as she stops to hug Sam and Holt. What the actual fuck is happening here. I clear my throat and she looks at me. They all look at me. "Hello, I'm Angie," she says holding her hand out to me. I take it and lean in close. God, she smells good. Like honey and oranges. I'm so hard I could break glass. I realize I've held her hand too long when she yanks it back.

"I'm Cody," I tell her.

"This is Cody Reynolds, the head football coach, retired NFL player for New York, and Super Bowl champ," Sam tells her but she just looks confused. Sam is clearly enjoying the fact that she has no idea who I am and that's fine. She will.

"Oh, you're Jim's son?" Well, if that doesn't chafe. So much for her being in this town for me. But she will be. She just doesn't know it yet. But she will be.

"Yeah, I am," I smile at her.

"Mind if I sit down?" She asks me in a breathy voice. And shit if I didn't almost come in my pants like a kid. Nodding, I scoot over so she can sit down. But not so far over that she has actual room. Nope, I am a big enough bastard that I left just enough room for her curvy ass so that her thigh has to be pressed to mine. Muahahaha. Insert evil villain laugh here. There's not even enough room on the seat for her purse, but she's polite so she just sets it on the floor next to her.

"What'll it be guys?" Katy asks us. "The usual?"

"What's the usual?" Angel asks.

"The biggest pizza we have with more meat on it than in a zoo, three dozen hot wings and a pitcher of beer," Katy laughs. Clearly amused with our disgusting man habits.

"Sounds amazing. Count me in too," she says, and I admire her confidence, no side salad for this one. Plus, my new life goal is to make sure she in takes enough calories to maintain that fantastic ass. Which is what I'm leaning back looking at when I hear Sam clear his throat. I look up and see his eyes are crinkled, his chest shaking as he silently laughs at me. Holt is mirroring Sam's hilarity. Bastards.

I can't stop looking at her. She's so god damn gorgeous. I wonder if she'd go out with me. I wonder what she looks like naked. I'm imagining what she looks like riding my cock, her full breasts bouncing in my face as she throws her head back when she comes. Jesus, I could come just thinking about what she looks like when she comes.

"Can I help you?" She asks me, a little annoyed. "Is there something on my face? Oh, God. Do I have a booger in my nose?" And nope, no, there is definitely nothing I can tell her in polite company right now. I feel my embarrassment at being caught burn across my tanned cheeks. I look over and those bastards' eyes are twinkling. Shit, they know what I was thinking.

"No, no. Nothing like that," I reassure her. Slightly. But what am I supposed to say? You're the most beautiful woman I have ever seen. No. I was wondering what you look like when you come. No, again. Shit, I'm such a creeper. "I was wondering if you'd like to go out sometime." There, I bit the bullet. I asked her out. I can feel how sweaty my pits are. Shit I hope I don't smell. When was the last time I was this hung up on a girl I really don't even know? If ever? I smell trouble, but my dick doesn't care.

"Let me get this straight, I don't know you, I work for your dad, you barely say two words to me the whole night over dinner, but sit there and creepily stare at me like a stalker and then you ask me out?" She asks, point blank. I can admire her candor. It's pretty sexy if I do say so myself.

"Yeah, that about sums it up," I tell her. Shit, she thinks I'm a loser. Which I am. What other fucker gets creamed at the end of the Super Bowl only to have his fiancée leave him for being a cripple and then hook up with the quarter back on the same team? A fucking loser, that's who. And a quick google search on her phone will confirm all of that so... She's studying my face and I hope to God she's kind when she shoots me down in front of my friends. I see the pitying looks on their faces and I know they see the same thing. Indifference, and then rejection in hers. My dick starts to wilt.

"Okay. When?" She asks. Shocking the shit out of all three of us. And just like that he pops right back up. We're back in the game, buddy, hang in there!

"What?" We all ask at the same time. She's not bothered at all by our moronic nature.

"When would you like to go out? I'd love to have someone show me the town. Aunt Mable just wants to hang out at the beauty shop, but I'm about forty years too young for that crowd," she says honestly, laughing softly. It's the best sound I have ever heard in the whole world. Shit. I'm such a loser.

"Is now too soon?" I ask and see Sam and Holt cringe. Too strong? Shit. I'm rusty. "How about Saturday night? We can grab dinner and drive around," I ask her.

"Great. It's a date," she smiles at me. Holy shit. I'm taking my angel to dinner on Saturday night. My mind starts to spin.

Cody

It's Saturday night and I'm ready. I am mother fucking ready. Look out, horse, I'm ready to get back on you. Oh, God, Sam is right, I'm such a douche. But I shake off those negative thoughts as I look at myself in the bathroom mirror. There is no place for that negativity here! My hair is a little long but I comb it. I've shaved my face, check. After shave, check. Deodorant, check. There are scars on my torso, but Holt says she's probably not going to see me naked for a while. While that sucks, I'm ok with it because for the first time in a long time, I want something. Someone. Plus, my abs are kind of the shit, so I'm hoping when Angel does see them, she doesn't care about the scars. Speaking of not seeing her naked for a while, new bottle of lotion in the bathroom, double sad face, check.

Is it warm in here? The towel around my waist is getting a little tight and scratchy. I look at the clock, no time. Shit. I have to make it go away. Baseball, nope. Cold showers, oh shit, I'm still hard. My grandmother wearing that flag bikini at the last Memorial Day BBQ at the lake. Aannnnndddd, I'm good. Whew, had to pull out the big guns on that one.

I look down at Steve, my German shepherd, is giving me a disgusted look. Steve would never go to this extent for woman, I just know it. But who does he think he is anyways. I shrug off his negativity.

"She's not like that, Steve," I tell him. "She's a nice girl." Steve just groans as he lays down.

Feeling like my time away from the flagpole is limited, I run to my closet and quickly step into some gray boxer briefs and my favorite worn too many times jeans. Shoving my dick in deep. That fucker needs to be secure. With the way my Angel gets to me, it'll only be a matter of time before I embarrass myself like I'm thirteen again. I throw on a black t-shirt and my brown leather belt and grab my socks and brown boots.

Steve just puts a paw over his eyes and groans again. Who knew he was such a judgey bastard. I run to my bureau and grab my wallet and cell phone and stuff them in my pockets. I palm my keys and head for the door.

Shit. I'm early. What to do, what to do? I grab my keys and run to my truck. I know what you're thinking. I have a big, shiny red truck to show off how tiny my dick is. And you would be wrong. I have an old beat up Chevy long bed that was my grandfathers and I worked my fingers to the bone and my body to near death on his farm to earn that old piece of shit. And I love it. And so does the old man. He laughs every time he sees me driving it.

I hop in my truck and head towards town. I see Ms. Maeve in her flower shop. I know she's about to close, so I jump out quickly and knock on the glass front door. When she hears me, she looks up and gives me the biggest smile. Ms. Maeve and my grandmother have been best friends since they were five years old. She waves to me to come in side.

I push open the door and she hustles around the corner to give me a big hug. I have to bend over because Ms. Maeve is all of about four foot ten and I'm about six foot four. She slaps my cheek playfully and smiles at my face smushed between her small, bony hands.

"Oooh! My precious boy," she squeals. "What are you doing in here with me? I hear you have a hot date with a certain New York nurse."

"That I do, Ms. Maeve, that I do. But I was hoping you had something befitting my angel," I smile back at her.

"I have just the thing," Ms. Maeve hurries over to the shop door and throws the sign to closed. Then she continues to flit around her store like the town's own personal flower fairy, which is something I've been trying to get her to admit to me since I was a little boy.

She spreads her special wax paper on her work table and runs over to the cooler on the left. She returns with a big tub of pink roses. I look at her. Roses? Aren't they a little overdone, a little valentine's day?

"Shut your mouth, child and let me work," she snaps at me without my ever uttering a word. "You pull up a stool and be a good boy."

"Yes, ma'am," I utter, chastised. And well, do as I'm told. I pull up an old, wooden stool and sit where many a bride has sat picking out flowers. Or many a man has sat, hoping to woo a girl. Is that what I'm doing? Wooing? Shit, now I'm rhyming. I'm such a pussy.

Ms. Maeve fidgets and fusses over the buds in her bucket before deciding on five pink roses that she lays on her work table. Then she flutters like a humming bird over to the cooler and deposits the bucket back in its place. Then she hops on over to the other cooler and nabs a bucket of big pink cabbages on stems and hurries back.

"Is that cabbage?" I ask. She shoots me a withering look.

"No, you moron, these are my precious peonies," she tells me with her chin in the air and her head held high. "You said you wanted something fitting an angel, well these are commonly known as angel cheeks." And I can't help but smile. Perfect. I make a mental note to find peony everything for my angel.

"That's perfect, Ms. Maeve. I knew my own flower fairy wouldn't let me down," I tell her as I round the corner and wrap my big arms around her, kissing her on the cheek.

"Oh, you big brute, turn me loose. I have important work to do. How do you expect to get laid if I can't get these flowers just right?" She says as she swats my chest.

"Ms. Maeve, I'm scandalized!" I tell her putting my hands over my ears as she shoots me a wink and laughs.

Next she replaces the peonies back in their rightful place after selecting the best, and moving on to choose some fern shit. Ferns? Like my gran has on her porch. Sure enough. This time I'm wise enough not to question.

Ms. Maeve starts to layer all of her different plant selections with her nimble fingers and I have to say, I'm impressed. If I had tried, it would have looked like shit. And I'm already getting enough guff from Steve. I don't need him thinking I'm a bigger loser than I already am. She deftly rolls the wax paper around the stems and greenery and ties a soft green bow around them to hold it all together.

"There you go, Champ. Go get your girl." She hands the bouquet to me and it's one of the prettiest things I've ever seen. Oh, God. I'm such a pussy.

"Thanks, Ms. Maeve. What do I owe you?" I ask her knowing full well what she'll say.

"Nothing. Don't you go and insult an old woman." Maeve has not let me pay for one thing in this shop my whole life. It would bother me more, but her husband Merle is a big oil baron.

Her shop is just to keep her from killing Merle now that he's retired and home all the time. "I thought your mama raised you better?" She play swats me again.

I kiss her cheek and make my way back out to my truck. I lay the blooms on the seat and fire the old girl up. I drive around the corner to the old blue craftsman on the main drag where I know Angel and Ms. Mable have set up shop. I get out of the truck and wipe my sweaty palms down my jeans. Oh, shit. What if Steve was right and I'm a moron? Jesus, I'm taking dating advice from a dog. I should have my head examined. Wait, I don't want to know. I reach in and grab my bouquet and head up the narrow walk. When I stop at the top, I take a deep breath to ease my nerves and knock on the door.

"Coming!" She shouts from in the house and God what I wouldn't give to hear her shout that under a different set of circumstances. I shake off the naughty thoughts because now is not the time to let my dick run the show, when the door opens to an angel, my Angel.

"Hi," I say softly. "These are for you." I hand her the flowers, my arm stiff, my head tipped down, shy. Oh, fuck. It's like I'm thirteen again.

"Hi," she smiles brightly at me. And reaches for the flowers. "Thanks for these. How did you know peonies are my favorite?" She leans in close and kisses my cheek. I can't help it, I wrap my right arm tight around her waist and hug her to me as she kissed me. I let go when she moves to step back.

"I didn't. But Ms. Maeve said they're called angel cheeks, and you're my angel, so I figured…" I trail off feeling like a tool.

"Well, I love them. Come on inside while I put them in water and grab my jacket," she says as she holds the door wide open. And not one to look a gift horse in the mouth, I follow her in like a lost puppy.

Angel makes her way towards the back of the house and into a bright, sunny kitchen. She sets my flowers on the counter gently. Almost, lovingly. Then heads over to a big white buffet cabinet. She opens the upper glass cabinet door and stands on her toes but can't quite reach what she wants. I make my way to stand behind her to see if I can see what she's looking for and, I can't be held accountable for what happened, it just did. I maybe leaned in a little too close. Her back to my front. My cock nestled lovingly between her cheeks. I bite my lip as I reach for the crystal vase she was reaching for.

Angel grabs onto the lip of the cabinet and holds on for dear life. She tips her head back against my shoulder and her eyes drift closed as I hear her breath catch in her throat. Maybe, my little Angel isn't as unaffected as she would like to have me believe. Things are looking up! I carefully lift the vase and set it on the counter area of the buffet, leaning in so my lips are right by her ear.

"Here you go, Angel," I say. My voice husky even to my own ears.

"Thanks," she croaks out. I take a step back and release her from the moment we seem to be caught in, this pull between Angel and me.

I see her steady herself with a deep breath and a naughty smile she throws me over her shoulder and I can't help but smile right back. She grabs the vase and heads over to the sink. Angel moves to the fridge and grabs a can of sprite and then makes her way over to the vase. She pops the can and dumps about a third of it in the vase and then offers the can to me.

"No thanks," I laugh.

"Suit yourself, but my pretty flowers will appreciate it," she fills the vase with water and carefully opens Ms. Maeve's ribbon and paper wrapping. Then delicately places her bouquet in the soda and water mix. Afterwards, tying the ribbon around her left wrist. "There. Ready to go?" She says studying her work.

"Yes, ma'am," I smile at her.

As she walks back toward the door, I really get a chance to look at her. Dark skinny jeans that could be second skin and a dark green, silky tank top that flows from her breasts just giving a hint of the glory that lies beneath. And Fuck me, she finishes it off with black heels. They're nothing special. Not the designer labels girls I dated in New York wore, but they are shiny and have a tall enough heel to make her ass look great.

It takes a minute for her to lock the old door once we're on the front porch and I reach around her with both arms to help shimmy the handle so the door with lock. I lead her down the walk to my truck and surprise her by opening her door for her.

"A gentleman? I thought you were a dying breed," she asks with a fake shocked face. I wink and shut her door behind her.

"Yes, ma'am," I tell her as I climb in and start the truck. "One of the last remaining."

"You're not what I was expecting," she tells me softly.

"And what were you expecting?" I ask her back.

"I'm not really sure. But I like what I see," she says softly.

The rest of the ride to the Bourbon Barrel, the best steak-house in Texas, and only twenty miles outside of town, passes in comfortable silence. Angel is a gal who doesn't need to fill silence nervously or awkwardly. I like that. I could almost see spending quiet nights at home with Angel and Steve, reading by the fire. Now where did that thought come from?

When we get to the Bourbon Barrel, I park the truck and quickly hop out and run around it to help Angel down. I offer her my arm as we walk into the restaurant and she takes it with a soft smile. I have a reservation and Maker's is in a town about as big as Tall Pines so everyone knows everyone. When we walk up to the hostess she grabs two menus and leads us to a quiet booth in the back.

"Here you go," then hands us our menus.

"Thanks, Amy," I tell her.

"Thank you," Angel tells her.

We study the menu for a while. I can't tell if she's a red wine or lager girl with her dinner. I'm about to ask her when she scares the shit out of me.

"Oh, this is a steak place?" She asks innocently. When I nod yes, she answers. "Damn, I guess I forgot to tell you, I'm a vegetarian."

And just like that my brain seizes. I let out a wheeze thinking well, it was nice knowing you, Angel of my dreams. How could I fuck up a date so badly before we even order drinks? Jesus.

"Got you!" She laughs. And I'm stunned. "Seriously, how rare do you think they can make it?" She asks in all seriousness.

"Wait, you're not a vegetarian?" I ask.

"No way. My mom was though. Hated the stuff. Felt we shouldn't eat animals. Mable and I always felt that they shouldn't be so delicious if we weren't supposed to eat them," she laughs and I can't help but laugh with her.

When the waitress shows up, we both order prime rib with loaded baked potatoes, broccoli with salads and a bottle of red wine to start. The food is amazing but the conversation is better. I can't believe how amazing Angel is. She's more. So much more. But I still can't bring myself to tell her that I remember her from the hospital in New York.

I don't tell her about the NFL and she doesn't ask which is nice. She does ask about my family and friends and how I like teaching at the school. She also loves the school and can't wait to see my team in action in the fall. I have a feeling that my boys will be seeing a lot of her as they're a pretty rough and tumble crowd.

"You ready to go, Angel?" I ask her softly after tossing a bunch of bills in the folder with the check. Her eyes have a happy soft, dreamy look to them. Whether it's from the wine, the food, or me, I don't care. I just love seeing it. Oh, who am I kidding? I hope it's me.

I walk Angel out to the truck and hold her door open for her. She smiles at me when I close it behind her. I round the hood and open my own door and hop in. Before I can even start the truck she's across the bench seat, snuggled into my side, her head on my shoulder.

"Cold?" I ask her.

"No," she tells me softly. I have to bite my bottom lip to keep from groaning as we make our way back into town. I park at the curb in front of her house and this time she doesn't make any pretense of trying to get out by herself. She knows it's important to me.

I open her door and take her hand to help her from the truck. She pulls her keys from her purse and unlocks the front door, but makes no move to open it.

"Thank you for a wonderful evening," she tells me as she reaches up to kiss me on the cheek. Like last time, I wrap my arms around her waist. But unlike last time, I turn my head at the last possible second and kiss her like I mean it. When she gasps, I run my hand up her back and into her long loose curls, licking into her mouth and tasting the red wine and Angel. When she sighs I soften my kiss and let go of her hair, but not her body. She lowers her eyes and rolls her bottom lip in her mouth, biting it while she gathers her thoughts.

"Want to come inside?" She asks me, her eyes meeting mine. And hell yes, I do. My dick has been harder than a goal post since the first time I saw my Angel, then and now, but I have to be sure.

Angellica

Want to come inside? I hear myself ask and it's like an out of body experience. But I can't help it. I have been aware of the handsome football coach since I first landed in this town, but tonight everything changed. He was kind and funny and surprisingly romantic. And let's not forget how sexy he is even if he isn't trying. So yeah, I invited him in.

"You sure?" He asks and I just smile coyly, I hope, and nod yes. "And Mable?" He asks.

"She's out of town," I tell him, my back to the door. He nods once, and tightens his grip on my waist. Like I said, sexy. He leans down and puts his forehead on mine.

"I'd love to," he says softly.

I turn and open the door. Placing my purse and keys on the table in the entry way. I hear Cody shut the door behind me and throw the lock. When I turn around, he's there, his mouth on mine. Cody lifts his hands and shoves them in my hair. And I go wild. I don't know what happened. I've never been like this before. With anyone. Not Joe. Not Jimmy the Saint Bernard. Not anyone in between.

Cody growls as he deepens the kiss. I wrap my arms around his neck and he lowers his hands to grab my ass and pull me tight against what is proving to be an impressive erection. Not one to look a gift horse in the mouth, I hop up and wrap my legs around his waist. I whimper when the stars align if you know what I mean. I throw my head back on my shoulders as he kisses his way down my jaw to that place on my neck that apparently makes me go crazy, I wouldn't know, no one has ever found it before. I grab fists full of his t-shirt in my hands and move my mouth back to his.

"Bedroom," he growls. "Where is your bedroom?" He demands as he slams my back up against the wall and kisses me again. I go a little dizzy for a minute when he pulls back and gives me that panty melting smile.

"Top of the stairs, to the left," I tell him as I wiggle my hips trying to get a little friction. Cody's grip on my hips tightens, pulling me harder against him and I whimper again.

His mouth comes back to mine as he tries to make his way to the stairs. I hear glass shatter and I know it was that ugly ass lamp Mable insisted on buying, but who cares. With sure feet, Cody carries me up the stairs and down the hall to my bedroom.

Once inside, the moon is shining through the sheer white curtains I have hanging in the three windows that make the rounded front of the house. Cody is even more handsome like this than I realized. I drop my feet to the floor and slowly push his t-shirt up over his chest. Cody reaches up behind him and grabs the back of the neck of his shirt and pulls it over head. He drops it to the floor and then kisses me again, his hands tangled in my hair.

His hands fall one by one from my hair to my shoulders, sliding straps of my silky tank off of my shoulders. The top floats down my body and settles around my heels. Carefully, I step out of my blouse and kick it to the side. I reach for Cody's belt, but he stops me before I can get it fully unbuckled. He finishes my task and pulls it free from his jeans, dropping it too to the floor. The whole time, his eyes are on me, on my body as he toes off his boots.

I step out of my black pumps and he looks sad to see them go. I unbutton my jeans and slowly lower the zipper. The sound deafening in my quiet, moonlit room. I push my jeans down my thighs and then step out of them when they are close enough to the floor to stand on the ends. I toss those out of the way too. Now, here I stand in nothing but a pink satin strapless bra with lace trim and matching panties.

That was apparently, all Cody needed. He grabs me again, kissing me hungrily. I gasp and he uses that to his advantage, licking his way into my mouth and I taste him and the wine. It's intoxicating. Running his hands up and down my back, my shoulders to my ass. He seems to shore up his courage because he reached for the clasp of my bra and unhooks it with skilled fingers. Cody tosses it to the side with one hand and quickly returns to my body, both hands sliding around to palm my breasts, lifting them. I scratch my nails down his abs, looking into his handsome face, and his hazel eyes are on my blue ones.

"You're beautiful, Angel," he tells me as he kisses the peak of one breast, his thumbs grazing over my nipples. "So fucking gorgeous," as he kisses the other. I moan and he takes my mouth again. I'm glad for it. I need him. Now.

Cody lifts me up in his arms again, but this time like a bride, as he carries me over and lays me on my bed. His body follows mine. His weight on his forearms by my head, caging me in, as his hips settle in between mine. Slowly putting pressure where I need him most as he kisses me slowly. Nipping at my lip and licking at my mouth. I groan, I need more. He just smiles against my mouth. Apparently the bastard is determined to take it slow.

He kisses his way down my jaw and over the spot on the side of my neck that makes me squirm. He smiles against my skin there too. His hands and mouth slowly making their way back to my breasts as he nips and kisses one breast, his index finger slowly circles my other nipple at a maddening pace. I try and wiggle underneath him to get some friction but I get nothing. When Cody chuckles against my breast, I snap.

"Quit playing," I tell him as I yank his head up by his hair.

"Oh, I've only just begun," he tells me as he starts to kiss his way back down my body. When he's kneeling between my thighs, his calloused hands peel my panties down my body and tosses them to the side of the bed. Before I know it, he's pushing my thighs wide and settling in between.

"Cody..." I start but I don't get any farther because there he is, his head between my thighs and it's amazing. I wiggle, but he has me pinned to the bed, opened for him. I can do nothing but take what he gives me. And he's definitely a giver. "Cody..." I say again. I'm close. So close. The tension is building in my body but I don't know what to do.

"Let go," he tells me and I do. As my back bows off the bed, my hands gripping the sheets that are knotted in my fingers, I whisper his name and let go.

As my breathing starts to slow, I open my eyes just in time to see Cody unbuttoning his pants and easing them and his boxers down his muscled legs. And what a show it is. And I was right, he is impressive. He slowly rolls a condom down over his hard length, my breath quickens. He's so beautiful. Scars and all.

"Baby..." He says, catching my attention from his cock.

"Hmm?" I ask distractedly.

"Baby..." He growls. "Angel, you can't look at me like that or this will be over too soon."

"Then come here," I tell him and he does.

He slowly climbs up the bed between my legs, looking at me like I've never been looked at. And I like it. He leans back over my body, crowding me again. His weight on his arms on either side of my face. His hips between mine. But this time so much better.

I wrap my arms around his middle, wiggling my hips against his. Cody leans down and kisses me hard, but sweet as he slides through my wetness. I hum in the back of my throat as he continues to slide back and forth. He drops his forehead to mine.

"Angel," he says on a whisper as he pushes all the way inside me. I arch into him, taking him fully.

"Yes," I tell him. Feeling the delicious stretch and burn as my body accommodates him.

"You're mine now," he says as he pulls back and plunges in.

"Yes," I gasp. He growls and his mouth finds mine again but this time harder, more demanding.

I dig my nails into his back as he thrust into me again and again. Kissing him back just as hard. He growls and reaches around his back to grab one of my arms and pull it back to the mattress clutched in his. I follow his lead and slide my other arm from around his back and up his other arm. Both my hands clutched in his to the mattress as he plunges in over and over. I moan. Its building. Again.

"Angel," he rasps as he picks up his pace. Faster and faster. Its building so fast I can't stop it. I don't want to.

"Yes."

"Come." And I do.

"Cody," I scream out his name as I do. He roars as he follows me over the edge, his fingers intertwined with mine.

I must have fallen asleep as I came down from what will be now known as the event. That moment when sex was more than just sex. With Cody it was amazing, it was everything. I know he felt it too. With a smile on my face, I reach over across the other side of the bed, but the sheets are cold. The house is so still, so quiet, I know I'm here alone. And I'm okay with that. We didn't make each other any promises. But damn, if it doesn't burn. I smell something sweet. I open my eyes, on the pillow next to mine is just one peony, one pink angel cheek. I grab the flower and clutch it to my chest as I fall back asleep, alone.

Cody

The minute I walked back in my house, I regretted it. I left my angel alone in her bed. And for the life of me, I can't remember why. Only that I just had to get out of there. Steve looks up from his doggie bed in the corner of my room, but that's it. He just raises his head and looks at me. I swear I saw him shake his head at me before laying it back down and going back to sleep. Granted, its three o'clock in the morning.

I step into my closet, a closet that feels huge, for the first time too big for one man. I kick off my boots and realize my belt is somewhere at Angel's. It'll probably be weird. Shit. I should apologize for being a tool. I strip off my socks and throw them in the hamper. I pull my t-shirt off to follow suit, but when it passes over my face, I smell Angel and me mixed together and I'm hard again. Fuck.

I strip my jeans off and head for bed, but when I get to it, I can't even bring myself to pull the covers back let alone climb in. Instead, I sit in the arm chair in the corner that faces my bed. I spend the next three hours imagining what Angel would look like in my bed. Her soft, blonde curls splayed out on my pillow. Watching her coming undone in my arms again. Her tiny body snuggled softly into my hard one as she sleeps with that little smile that plays on her face. Shit.

I'm losing my mind. I drop my head into my hands and for some reason, want to cry. It was one night, one date. Why am I so bent out of shape over the fact that I probably fucked everything up by sneaking out? Why did the thought of staying scare the shit out of me so bad?

Six o'clock rolls around and I'm still awake so I know what I have to do. I stand up and walk back into my closet, stripping out of my boxers as I go. I grab my favorite pair of running shorts. The short little ones that make all the girls tongues fall out when they see them. But that's not why I wear them. They are so freaking comfortable. I tie the little string tight because, I don't need a wardrobe malfunction in the town I grew up in. I'm still relatively famous so you know that shit would end up on the internet.

I grab my favorite running shoes and lace up. A couple of deep quad stretches and some calf stretches. I roll my shoulders and head out into the early morning gray. Nothing like ten grueling miles to get your heart pumping and clear your head.

I open my front door and am greeted by Steve who is holding his leash in his mouth. This is his passive aggressive attempt to tell me I forgot something this morning. Or really, someone. Namely, Steve.

"Oh, so now you like me," Steve just wags his tail. Fluffy bastard will do anything for a run. "Ok, buddy. Let's go," Steve jumps up. I quickly clip his leash to his collar and head back out, this time my furry buddy in tow.

Steve and I do another three miles. He easily keeps up with me. We've been running every day since he was a pup. He helped me get back on my feet more than he will ever know. Or, maybe he does. Either way, I love him.

When we get back, Steve and I both head to the kitchen for a much needed water break followed by some more deep stretches. Ok, I stretched, he flopped down on his living room doggie bed and took a deep nap. I followed up with a trip to my weight room and spent the rest of the late morning making the rest of my body ache the way my heart did. That afternoon, after I showered, I really lived it up and did my laundry.

For dinner, I pan grilled chicken breast with tomatoes and spinach and had a little brown rice on the side. Man, I am just a party a minute. But while my Sunday was anything but fun, I have a plan. I am going to talk to Angel first thing in the morning. So, tonight, Steve and I head to bed for a good night's sleep.

What a bunch of bullshit. I don't think I have ever not slept this much in my entire fucking life. I'm pretty sure Steve is plotting my death for keeping him up all night with my tossing and turning. It's like my brain just wouldn't turn off. I pretty much hate myself. Yesterday, I was so busy, I didn't have time to doubt my plan to make Angel see that I'm an idiot and I deserve another chance. Now, I'm a fucking mess.

I get up before my alarm and shut it off. Steve and I head out for another quick run but it does little to improve my mood. Steve is glowering at me for ruining his run.

When we head into the kitchen for a water refresher, I look at the coffeepot and briefly consider just pouring the pot straight down my throat.

I make my way into my bathroom, stripping of my workout gear as I go, and turn the water to hot, but quickly change my mind. I let out a less than manly shriek as I stepped into a shower of water that had to come straight from the Arctic Tundra. As I soap up, I picture Angel's small,but strong hands on my body again in my mind. This is not helping my situation. A man's gotta do what a man's gotta do. And if that man wears athletic pants and a football polo every day to work to coach teenage boys who are very sex crazed, that man does not show up to work with a woody. So, this man, takes matters into his own hand. Literally. I wrap my hand around my cock and remember Angel's soft body, her needy cries for more. I brace myself against the shower wall with my other hand and in an embarrassingly short number of strokes, I pop off like a rocket. The sad thing is, I'm still half hard. Well, a half chub is better than a full one I guess.

I quickly rinse back off and step out of the shower. I towel off and head to my closet. I make quick work of my work uniform. Black track pants with black athletic stripes down the sides of the leg over my gray boxer briefs, and a teal polo with the War Eagle logo on them. Teal doesn't exactly say tough and manly to me, but I don't make the rules, I just coach the kids. I lace up my running shoes and clip my school ID badge to my hip. I put my wallet and cell phone in my pockets and grab my keys. I eat a speedy breakfast and head out the door.

"Don't do anything I wouldn't do, Steve!" I shout on my way out but he just groans and goes back to sleep.

The drive to the school is relatively short and before I know it, I am pulling my truck into my spot in the parking lot and majorly chickening out. Shit.

First period is spent conditioning our varsity team. Sam and I stand on the sidelines of the track watching the boys run wind sprints.

"So…." Sam starts, laughter in his eyes. "I heard you took our sexy nurse out Saturday night," he tells me.

"You already know this. You were there when I asked her out," I tell him checking my watch for the kids' times.

"I also heard your truck was parked in front of her house until really really early in the morning." This, I also knew, but didn't know was common knowledge. Granted, sometimes this town is about as big as a postage stamp so anything is possible.

"If you already know, why are you asking me?"

"Because you are not looking like a man who had his world rocked by nurse sin," I groan. "In fact, you're looking pretty pitiful," he tells me.

"Because I ran. At like three o'clock in the morning. And now I'm fucked."

"Well, maybe you can talk to her about it, instead of being a chicken shit," he tells me. And he's right, I am being a chicken shit. But now, I know I fucked up. What if I try to apologize, try for more and she rejects me. In my head I know that would hurt so much more than the betrayal Kimmy dished out in New York.

The rest of the day passes with my coaches and I running training drills with the kids, and then meetings about how we want to form and train our team for next year. There is a lot of pressure on us to take the team all the way to state this year. I would love to see the boys accomplish that. I know they can if they just work hard enough.

By the time lunch rolls around, I'm pretty much done for the day. I grab a chicken salad sandwich and a coke from the cafeteria and make my way to the staff lounge. I see my dad and Sam and head on over to their table.

"Hey, dad, how's it going?" I ask him. My dad is the best guy I know. I love seeing him every day and honestly, I don't know what would have happened to me if he hadn't offered me this opportunity.

"Can't complain. Sam and I were just talking about how this year's team is shaping up. He said you guys have great prospects and a great summer training program in place."

"That we do," I say, taking a bite of my sandwich.

"Now, what is this bullshit I hear about you blowing things with Nurse Angie?" He asks me. I shouldn't be surprised, my dad has been this direct my whole life. He gets it from my grand-parents. I cough trying to swallow the big bite of sandwich in my mouth. It's turned to sawdust so I can't get it down, but I keep trying all while glaring at Sam. Sam the Betrayer. That is how I shall now refer to him.

"You're fired," I tell him when I can finally talk. But Sam just laughs.

"Dude, you can't fire me. And stop being such a pussy. Have you even talked to her yet?" He asks me.

"No," I say quietly, my head hanging down.

"What was that?" Sam asks. The asshole.

"I said no you bastard," I growl finishing my sandwich as quickly as possible, I ball up my trash. I'm eager to get away from these two conspirators.

"Well, Sam is right, you can't fire him," my dad tells, like I don't already know. I "fire" him at least once a week. "Second, look around you. She's not in here. Probably afraid it would be awkward. So, son, I say this with love, but grow a set and go talk to the first good woman you have been interested in before she tosses your sorry ass out in the street." Well, how does he really feel?

And the big pussy that I am, that is exactly what I do. I grab my trash and toss it in the trash can before making my way to the door. All to the tune of my coaching staff and my dad sing-ing "Some Day My Prince Will Come," I pause, with my hand on the door and look over my shoulder at those idiots. I really do love them. I shake my head and then flip them the bird over my shoulder which is met with chuckles and head down the hall to the nurse's office.

Outside her office, which is really two giant offices and a bathroom enclosed in one giant area, I take a deep breath to shore up my courage, square my shoulders and knock on the door.

"Come in," she tells me.

When I walk through the door, she's seated at her desk, reading a magazine. The nurse's desk is in the middle of the first big room, surrounded by cabinets on two walls full of I don't know what, a bathroom on the third wall, and bulletin boards covered in flyers and pictures of students, calendars and various school debris. To her left is a big medical curtained entry way that leads to the second big room that is four bays with medical tables and curtain dividers.

"Any patients?" I ask, nodding my head to the curtain.

"No, it's been a slow day, but you know what they say, no news is good news," she smiles at me.

"Angel…" I say at the same time she speaks.

"Cody, are you alright?"

"I don't know," I tell her. She stands up from her chair and starts walking towards me. "I feel like I need to apologize for the other night." Her face falls. Shit this isn't working out.

"Okay," she tells me. "You don't have to apologize. It's been a long time. I'm out of practice. And well, Joe cheated with slut Erin so, you know. I'm sure he had his reasons," she tells me as she breaks my fucking heart. She's babbling. She thinks she doesn't do it for me and she couldn't be more wrong.

"Angel…" I start but she cuts me off.

"Please don't call me that. My name is Angie," she hurries on. "And it's ok, really. But I'd like to still be friends." And I fucking snap. I throw the lock on the door.

"I don't want to be friends, Angel," I growl as I stalk towards her. Her face falls but only for a minute. I back her up against her desk, my hips pinning hers roughly. I grab a fist full of her hair and hold her still for my punishing kiss. Friends? No fucking way. Angel. Is. Mine.

"Cody?" She asks tentatively when I let her mouth go. Kissing her jaw and that place on her neck that makes her lose her mind. For me.

"I don't want to be friends, Angel, because you are mine," I hear her breath hitch as she grabs onto my shoulders. I take her mouth again as I unbutton her jeans, pushing both her pants and her panties down around her ankles. I run my fingers between her legs and she's wet. Fucking soaked for me. Angel lets out that little mewl that makes me crazy.

I turn her around to face away from me and guide her down so that she's folded over, her beautiful chest mashed against her desk. I make quick work, freeing myself from my pants and shorts. I take her lush hips in both hands and plunge inside her. Deep. She turns her head to the side and I see her bite her lip to keep from screaming out as I pump in and out.

"You're mine, Angel."

"Yes," she whispers.

"Say it," I thrust in again. This time harder. "Say. It," I command.

"Yes," She tells me. "I'm yours."

"Damn right," I tell her as I pick up my pace. I feel her grip my dick so tight. I know she's getting close. I slide my left palm over her full ass and up her spine, laying it flat between her shoulder blades over her blouse. My right hand wraps around her hip to where her body takes mine and I feel it on my fingertips. I growl over how hot our connection makes me. When my fingers find that spot on her body, I circle it, hard. Not letting up as I thrust harder, faster. She's so close and thank God, because I am walking a knife's edge right now over her body.

"Cody…" She breathes my name and it is the sexiest thing I have ever heard. My angel claws at her desk as she comes. Her face flushing. I pump my hips once, twice before I come. Hard.

"Angel," I tell her as I kiss her shoulder before I stand, slipping from her body has never felt more wrong. I tuck myself back in my pants and look down as she's sprawled over her desk panting. I pull her panties up her legs and then her jeans, dressing her gently.

When she catches her breath, Angel stands up on shaky legs. Sitting in her chair before she falls. She looks up at me with those big blue eyes, questioning me, everything, what just happened between us. But it's more. So much more.

"Cody?" She asks.

"I made a mistake, Angel," I watch as her face falls and quickly tip her chin up to look at me, tears shimmering in her eyes. "Not you, baby. Not us. Never us. I got scared and I left you in the middle of the night. Not because you weren't everything I expected, but because you were so much more." And in her eyes, I see hope.

"Okay," she tells me and I smile before kissing her lips.

"Okay," I tell her. I kiss her one more time. "Tonight. Dinner. My place. Pack a bag," I tell her as I make my way to the door of her office.

She smiles at me and nods. She'll be there. In my house. In my bed. All night. I can't wait. That hope in her eyes is contagious. I can't help but hope.

"Oh, and bring your running shoes. Steve loves to run," I tell her.

"Running shoes?" She questions. "Steve?"

"Steve the Pirate, my dog. Loves to run. Oh, and word to the wise, don't stare at his eye, he hates that," I tell her. "Until tonight, Angel." I tap the door jamb twice, my A&M ring clinking against the wood as I do. And then head out the door. I've got a lot to do before tonight. It's time to make a stand.

Angellica

To say the rest of the day passed in a blur would be accurate. Once Cody left my office, I had a lot to think about. Cody is definitely keeping me guessing. One minute he's in it, the next he bails. Only to come back, and then he's claiming me, and it was hot, now he's leaving again but with the promise of a date with him and his dog tonight. All the while, I'm sitting here in my office at my new job with dirty panties. And I'm not really sure how I feel about that.

I meant it when I said it was a slow day. No more students visited me for any reason the rest of the day. I busied myself by making sure the kids in the incoming ninth grade were up to date on their immunizations. What can I say? My life is glamorous. Then I sent an e-mail to the Principal to see if we could offer to inoculate graduating seniors who were going away to college for a whole host of disgusting things they would be exposed to living in dorms. That reminds me, the football coaches teach health class. I should talk to Cody about their

Sex Ed classes. I put a pin in the wrap the banana chat for later. Which also reminds me he did not use one in my office, so that talk is probably more urgent than usual.

By the time the bell rings, I am ready to blow this Popsicle stand. I grab my purse out of the bottom drawer of my desk and head for the parking lot. Since leaving the city and moving to small town Texas, I had to buy a car. Jim, my boss, told me not to get a girly car or I would regret it come the flooding and possible snow, and his wife, Emily, told me as sad as she was to admit it, he was right, so I took my savings down to the car dealership in town and bought myself a cute little Jeep Grand Cherokee. It's white with gold trim and has all the bells and whistles including, but not limited to four wheel drive, satellite radio, and a GPS that yells at me more often than not. Unfortunately, Aunt Mable borrowed my car to go to the market before her car got here and she changed it to an Englishman who cusses. She laughed a blue streak about it, so I let her keep it. Really, and if you repeat this, I'll deny it until the day I die, I cannot figure out how to change it back.

I head home, thankful for the time to clean up and pack a few things. I pull into the drive way and take off for my room like I'm Usain Bolt. Maybe I can run? Shit. Who am I kidding, I am totally going to embarrass myself. I run into my room and toss my work clothes into the hamper on my way into the shower. I might have just set the land speed record for showers when I step out and towel off.

I already had my long curly hair piled up in a messy bun on top of my head so I will leave it that way for my run with Cody and Steve the Pirate. I throw on gray marbled yoga capris and a gray yoga tank that's cut low in the back and sides and shows off the built in aqua sports bra. I round the look out with ankle socks and my running shoes, which is a joke. Does this body look like I run? Hell, no! I do yoga, that's also why I'm so flexible when I need to be, if you know what I mean.

I run back to my closet and pull out my purple carryon bag, this should be just the right size. I toss in a short red pleated silk skirt with little white flowers all over it and a white sleeveless collared shirt that buttons up the front. I add a skinny gold belt and nude patent leather flats. Panties and a bra because that would be super embarrassing to forget, and super inappropriate because I work with children. I run to the bathroom and grab my toiletries bag out of the cabinet and toss in my toothbrush deodorant, face wash, and makeup bag. Jesus, I need a lot of shit to look good. Shit. I should probably pack pajamas. It's probably a little presumptuous to sleep naked and that feels a little weird anyway. I run back to my dresser and grab my favorite night gown. It's just a white cotton spaghetti strap number with a lace hem, but it's comfortable, and I think it's pretty. I grab two extra pairs of panties because Cody is proving to be a wild card. I zip up my bag and head for the door. Aunt Mable is at her showing, so I don't have any questions to answer.

I grab my keys and purse from the table by the door and check my phone. Cody has texted me his address, so I plug it into the GPS in my jeep after I stow my bag in the trunk and my purse on the seat next to me.

Cody lives just outside of town. And when I say just outside of town I mean his long ass driveway is in town but his house, his property, is not. I see how he runs in town all the time. The white horse fencing is gorgeous and goes on for as long as the eye can see. In the distance there is a large yellow farmhouse that is gorgeous. Another white Victorian sits off to the right of the gate, but in the back, visible from the gate, but about five miles back is a log cabin with wrap around porch. That is my destination. I briefly wonder if my boss lives in one of the houses towards the front of the property, but shake the idea off. It will only serve to make me more uncomfortable and awkward.

I park my jeep next to Cody's truck and get out, grabbing my purse and palming my keys. When I look up, Cody is standing on the front porch, scowling at a one eyed German shepherd who is so cute he is positively smiling! But why does Cody look so pissed.

"Hi," I say shyly. Steve thumps his tail on the porch and Cody scowl deepens.

"Hi," he says abscnt mindedly.

"Is everything alright?" I hedge.

"Maybe?"

"Ummm…" Did he change his mind? Shit. I should go. At least I didn't pull my overnight bag out of the trunk yet. Then I'd really look like a tool. "Umm, I'll just go…" I trail off.

"What?!" Cody looks up at me for the first time since I arrived looking…upset. Steve looks downright murderous…At Cody! "Why would you leave?"

"Well, you look unhappy. I thought maybe you changed your mind," I tell him.

"No. NOOO! Come on in. Wait, where's your bag?"

"In the trunk," I tell him.

"Let me get that real quick, why don't you get to know Steve. Remember what I said," he warns.

I walk up the three steps to the porch where Steve is sitting, his tail is wagging so hard we could use it to create wind power. And I swear the dog is smiling at me. I hold my hand out, palm up and let him sniff me, get to know me. Before he leans forward, closing his good eye and tips his nose down so that I can pet him.

"Well, hello, sweet boy," I coo. "My name is Angie. Thank you for being nice to me. I've never been around dogs before, let alone big, strong handsome boys like you." He wags his tail some more and pants.

"Unbelievable," Cody mumbles and I look up confused. "I swear, he barely tolerates me and here you are and he's all over you."

"He is not," I argue, but Steve's chin is resting on my shoulder and I am still crouched down in front of him with my arms wrapped around him. I'm dating Cody and I haven't even kissed him yet, I guess this could be weird. Cody carries my bag into the house and waits for Steve and me to enter.

"Come on, buddy, let's go make the grouch happy," I tell Steve and he chuffs in agreement. Cody just grumbles.

Cody drops my bag by the stairs and moves to grab Steve's leash from the hook by the door. I take a minute to look at him, really look at Cody. He's in running shorts and a Texas A&M t-shirt that is so old and faded it has to be a favorite. The shirt is stretched tight across his back muscles. He seems to fancy the shorty running shorts, and looking at his long muscular legs and firm backside, I can't say that I disagree. I hear him clear his throat and look up to see him looking over his shoulder at me from where he's bent over Steve, hooking his leash to his collar.

"See something you like, Angel?" He asks me, his voice husky.

"Maybe," I say shrugging my shoulders, but Cody just throws his head back and laughs. He is so handsome when he laughs. Like little bits of him from before the accident come out. Oh, and I know about the accident, and I know who he is. I would have recognized him anywhere, but the last thing I want to do is bring up painful memories.

"Alright, let's do some stretches to warm up," he tells me. He starts doing calf and quad stretches while I do a quick run through of my favorite yoga moves.

"Do you run often?" He asks me.

"Do I look like I run often?" I glare at him.

"So what do you do to keep in such fantastic shape?" He asks distractedly. I've just risen from a downward dog/ upward facing dog movement.

"Yoga," I answer, looking at him like he's suffering from a head trauma. "Obviously."

"Hmm?" He asks. Watching me move through sun salutations.

"Yoga," I say again. "I do yoga."

"So that's why you're so bendy," he says as he swoops in and lifts me off my feet. I land on my back on the couch with Cody on top of me. I squeal as he tickles my sides but my laughter is cut short when his mouth finds mine and he kisses me soundly.

"We should go run," I tell him, breathlessly.

"We don't need to run tonight," Cody tells me with all seriousness. Steve growls from the corner.

"If you want to live to see tomorrow, I suggest we take Steve for his run," I tell them both. Steve chuffs his approval, Cody scowls. "You're a big boy, you'll survive an hour," I tell Cody as I pat his cheek. He scowls again, I just laugh.

As it turns out, Steve really loves to run. We jogged about two miles at my slow pace. I urged Cody to do his real run which was a ten mile killer. I'd be dead before dinner if we did that. It was mutually agreed upon by both Steve and Cody that Steve would stay with me for safety reasons. And also he knew his way home in the dark. Something, I did not.

Steve was happy to go at my slower pace. He ran the whole time with his tail and nose high in the air, the former wagging the whole time. I kind of wanted to wag my tail too. Steve was great company. Maybe I needed a pet.

Even though Steve and I had a much shorter run than Cody's death march, at my much slower pace, we still beat him home. Out of shape and gasping for air as we made the final feet of our run. Up the steps where I dropped to the porch and collapsed on my back, arms open wide, legs spread eagle. I think Steve feels for me as I lay there looking like road kill, my face red and sweat pouring off my body, because he groaned his doggie groan as he too, flopped to the porch and rolled over onto his back with his legs in the air and his tongue lolling out to the side of his mouth. My hand stretched out absent mindedly rubbing his belly. And this is how Cody found us when he returned from his run.

I could hear his footfalls bringing him closer, but I couldn't bring myself to care. I was fairly sure I died somewhere on that run and my body just didn't figure it out until we got back to the house.

"You need to stretch again," he tells me with his foot on the railing, stretching his own body.

"Ungh," is all I can get out. See? Dead. Cody just laughs.

I feel his strong fingers wrap around my ankle and lift my leg, straight up in the air, pushing my knee as far towards my face as it can go. I've been practicing yoga since I was a teen so there is no push back from my muscles and joint. Add to that the fact that all my muscles have quit on me and I have the consistency of over cooked spaghetti, I am very flexible right now. I grab that ankle from him and pull it all the way over my head. I hear him make a strangled sound in the back of his throat but disregard it.

I let that leg fall back to the ground and Cody wraps his strong hands around my other ankle, lifting it straight up. Once I can reach it myself, I grab that ankle and pull it over my head. I'm so tired, my eyes remain closed the whole time. Once I lower that leg back to the ground, I continue to relax in corpse pose, I could probably fall asleep right here.

"Get in the house, Angel," Cody growls. My eyes instantly snap open.

"What?" I whisper.

"I said, Get. In. The fucking. House," he ground out between his teeth. "Now."

"Cody…" I start. "Did I do something wrong?"

"Unless you want me to fuck you on the front porch in front of both my parents and my grandparents. Get. In. The fucking. House. Angel."

"Oh," I say, because well, he really paints a picture.

"Yeah, oh," he snaps back. And now that I look at him, I see his control crumbling away. So I hold out my hand for him to help my broken body up off the floor of the porch.

"Okay," I say softly. Rolling his eyes skyward, Cody mumbles something that resembles curses and counting. But before I can say anything, he grabs my hand to help me up, but once I'm vertical again, he just keeps lifting and lifting until he tosses me over his shoulder like a sack of potatoes and into the house we go. Yippee!

Cody

I spent my whole run thinking about Angel. Usually, I use my runs to clear my head, but lately, she is always on my mind. This is as concerning as it is fantastic. She's beautiful, she's smart, and she's funny. Hell, even my dog is crazy about her and I'm still not even sure he likes me. I can't help but feel like I'm falling for her and that seems crazy. I could easily make her mine tomorrow.

I'm more protective of Angel than I ever thought I could be towards another person. It was like asking me to tear off my own arm when she said she was going to turn around and head back but that I should continue my normal run at my normal pace. I wouldn't have agreed if she didn't take Steve with her. He might only have one eye, but he could be a killer if he needed to. And what about how Kimmy treated me? She ripped my heart out when I was at my weakest. I never sold her engagement ring. Not because I hoped she would reconsider, but to have a physical reminder of how much a woman can hurt you. How much damage they can do. Can I let Angel in? To give her the chance to crush me? As much as I want to, I'm not sure I can. And even if I do, what will happen when she finds out about the secret I have been keeping from her, because secrets always have a way of coming out of the dark. How will she feel about me then?

I hate this dark turn my thoughts have taken, but I just can't help it. I know what Kimmy and I had wasn't real. But in my head and in my heart, I know things with Angel are the real deal. God, I'm such a pussy. Sam and Holt would laugh their asses off if they heard me like this.

I try and shake off these weird moods and girly emotions as I pass through the gate of my family homestead. I love this place. I love the farmhouse my parents raised me in and still live in to this day. I love the old Victorian built by my great great grandfather for his bride that my grandparents, my dad's parents, still live in. And I love the old cabin that is mine. It was once the original homestead and a real piece of shit on the inside seeing as no one had lived there for over a hundred years. So while I was still in the NFL I gutted the house myself and brought her back to her glory, and then some, in between seasons. It turned out to be perfect because I had a place to land after my injury. Add to that the job my dad had offered me in the hospital and I had the tools I needed to rebuild my life.

I'm just rounding the lane that leads to my cabin when I see my dog and my girl sprawled on the porch like roadkill. I can't help the smile that over takes my face. It's almost painful. Jesus, when was the last time I really smiled. Really laughed. I hit the base of the steps and there they are, Angel on her back like a starfish, arms and legs wide, eyes closed. Steve is also on his back, but his four doggie legs are straight up in the air, his tongue is hanging out of his furry face.

"You need to stretch," I tell her as I put my leg up on the porch railing to stretch out my muscles. Angel just groans which draws my attention to her as I switch legs.

I look at her, really look at her. Her little workout outfit is adorable. I didn't figure her for a jogger, but she caught me off guard with that yoga comment. She's still laying on the porch, panting. Her heavy breathing makes her full breasts bounce with each breath. The cool evening air is chilling her over heated skin causing her nipples to stiffen. I don't even think she notices. Her skin is flushed and glowing with sweat. This is exactly how she looks after I take her. And suddenly, that's all I can think about.

Trying to rally my thoughts, I wrap my hand around her ankle and lift it up towards her body to stretch out her leg. Two thirds of the way towards her face, with no sign of stopping, Angel surprises the hell out of me and pulls her ankle over her head and holds it there for a few seconds before releasing it. I let out a strangled gurgle watching her do the splits on her back. I think I'm suddenly a big fan of yoga.

I grab her second leg, not wanting her to hurt herself, yeah, that's what we're going to go with. And not that I want her to do it again. I lift her leg towards her head and again, she takes over, taking her ankle above her head, holding it there for a while, before releasing it back to the ground. Then, as if she couldn't surprise me more, I watch her start to drift off to sleep on my front porch with a smile on her face and the mother of all hard-ons in my pants. For the first time in my life, I am glad that the cabin sits back farther behind the other two houses. The last thing I need either my mother or my gran see is the giant tent I pitched in my favorite running shorts. Or worse, the thought of taking my sweet Angel on the porch is suddenly appealing.

"Get in the house, Angel," I growl because I need her. Now. Like a cat in the sun, she just wants to be left to sleep but that just isn't happening. Not since I saw her sweaty and panting on my porch. Now, I want to see her sweaty and panting in my house. Naked. Underneath me. On top of me. The list is endless.

"Unless you want me to fuck you on the front porch in front of both my parents and my grandparents. Get. In. The fuck-ing. House. Angel." I'm barely hanging on to my control by a thread and I think she gets that because she reaches up a sweet little hand for me to help her limp body up off of the floor. I grab her hand but pull her up over my shoulder and stalk to the front door.

I throw the door open and Steve walks in. He makes his way to the kitchen for his water and dinner which are already there for him. Then he will nap on the doggie bed in the living room. I take the stairs two at a time with my naughty little nurse over my shoulder and stalk my way to my bedroom door, slamming it behind me. I think Steve will stay down stairs, but nothing kills a mood like a one hundred and twenty five pound, one eyed dog staring at you while you make love to your woman.

I carry Angel into the master bathroom and slowly slide her down over my shoulder, down my body so she can feel every inch how turned on I am. She opens her eyes and I see the heat in them as she looks at me. Then I take her mouth. I could kiss her for days. But not now. Now I need her too much. I pull her little tank over her head and growl when I see she has no bra on underneath, it was one of those built in thingies girls wear, but now she's bare to me and it does something to me. It. Makes. Me. Wild.

I pull my t-shirt over my head and toss it the way Angel's went to the floor. Next, I strip her shoes and socks off her little feet. Tossing them in the same direction. Angel reaches for my dick in my shorts, but I catch her wrist in my hand and shake my head no just once. Hoping to convey the fact that if she touches me, this will be a hard and fast fuck, but I want so much more.

I strip her tight pants down her legs and have to grab my dick to keep from coming as she steps out of them, one foot at a time. I pick her up by her waist and sit her on the bathroom counter in between the two sinks on the cool granite top. Without hesitation I plunge two fingers into her tight pussy and she moans and grabs onto my shoulders. Angel throws her head back as I curl my fingers inside of her. I swallow down her cries as I kiss her again. And when I feel like she's close, I pull my fingers from her body and walk to the shower to turn the water on.

I strip my shorts down my legs, and stalk naked, back to Angel, who is reclining against the mirror, her eyes closed and her gorgeous chest heaving with each glorious breath she takes. She doesn't notice my approach as I drop to my knees in front of the vanity and pull her hips to the edge of the counter.

I lick her once and she sucks in a deep breath and screws her eyes shut. I lick her twice and her fingers squeeze the stone edge of the counter so hard, I'm surprised it doesn't crush in her grip. I seal my mouth over her and she gasps as she calls out my name. God, I love the sound of that.

"Cody," she says again as I thrust my two fingers in her core and curl them like before. One of her hands finds its way into my hair and she pulls. Hard. I almost come right there, but manage to hold back. Just barely. And then she comes. And comes. And it's so beautiful to watch.

When she comes back down to earth, I pick her up and carry her into the now steamy shower. Her legs wrapped around my waist, her arms around my shoulders with her face nuzzled into my neck. My hands are on her ass as I lean her into the stone shower wall so I can shut the glass door. Angel is kissing my neck as the steam swirls around us. Her soft, warm, wet body sliding against my cock. But it's when she bites my ear that I lose my mind.

Pinning Angel to the shower wall, I hold her over the tip of my cock and slam her down on it. We both groan out loud. She circles her hips and there goes the ballgame, folks. I pull back and slam into her. Again and again. There are no words. No yeses or I loves yous. Just hot, heavy breaths as I take her against the hard shower wall.

Angel squeezes her eyes tight again and wraps her arms around me, her face in my neck as she comes again. But I'm not done with her, not by a long shot. I pick up my pace and thrust into her tight body, harder, faster.

"Again," I bark out. Its building. I can tell the way her body grips mine. She's close but not there yet.

"Cody," she breathes.

"Touch yourself," I tell her. "Now." Without hesitation, she lets go of my neck with one arm and slides her hand down her belly to where our bodies join together and circles.

"Cody." She's close, desperate for it and so am I. I pound into her even harder.

"Faster, baby." I'm so close but so is she. She throws her head back against the stone wall of the shower.

"Cody." She's there. She closes her eyes.

"Look at me," I demand. And those baby blues instantly pop open. The moment is so intimate. So intense. And she looks at me as she touches herself as I fuck her against the shower wall. And then she comes on a scream that I swallow down my throat as I kiss her. I thrust into her once, twice more before I come harder than I ever have before into her warm body.

We're both still breathing hard when I pull from her body and slowly lower her feet to the shower floor. Gently, I shampoo her hair and wash the sweat from her body. And hell, if I'm not half hard again watching my come roll down her legs, but I've worn her out. It wouldn't be fair to take her again even though my body wants to. Twice today, I didn't use a condom. Before,

I would be ready to slit my own throat for my stupidity, but all I can think about is how gorgeous she'll be when her belly is round with my baby. I need to shut that shit down right now. Clearly, I've lost my mind.

When we're both washed up, I shut the water off and towel us both dry. I pull on a pair of boxer briefs and take one of my t-shirts and drop it over her head. Then I take her hand and lead her down stairs to the kitchen where I wow her with my cooking skills. At least I hope.

We sit together at my battered oak kitchen table, smiling at each other over the grilled chicken breast and cooked spinach I made for dinner. I laughed when she turned her nose up at it. As it turns out my sexy nurse might keep her body toned with yoga, but that's where her healthy streak ends. Her idea of eating a vegetable is mushrooms on her pizza. Her genetics are truly amazing.

After dinner, we wash the dishes together, side by side at the sink. When we're done I take her hand and lead her up the stairs back to my bedroom where I strip my shirt off of her and make love to her slowly, sweetly, with her hands in mine. Afterwards, I curl my body around hers. Her back to my front. And fall into the deepest, sweetest sleep I have ever had in my life. I am so screwed.

TEN

Angellica

Three Weeks Later...

The last couple of weeks have passed in a blur. A beautiful blur of Cody and I both working at the school, meeting up for runs and dinner, going out on weekends with our friends or just us, and delicious sex. It's been so good. We have dinner with Aunt Mable at least once a week. Cody even took me to her showing in Dallas one weekend. But I'm tired. Actually, I'm fucking sick.

Two weeks ago, I had a rash of students with fucking strep and mother fucking bronchitis. I should have known this would happen. What the fuck is wrong with me. Actually, I know what's wrong with me. I was so wrapped up in my yummy sexy, sexy time bubble of sin that I didn't get enough rest and vitamin C or whiskey, whatever. I took all the precautions I would have in the hospital, but all my efforts proved to be futile. I'm fucking sick.

So, here I am on a Monday, laying on the floor underneath my desk in the fetal position praying for a quick death before I cough so hard I pee my pants. Or vomit. Or both.

Cody and I spent the weekend apart because he and Sam and the other coaches were away at a coach's clinic. And thank God for small favors. Steve spent the weekend with Cody's parents. I spent it hoping to die but not actually doing it.

I hear foot steps outside my office and I pray to pizza and bourbon and hot romance cover model gods that this person keeps on going. I should have known better. I haven't seen Cody in four days. I knew that sweet bastard was going to check in. Gah! A knock falls on my door and I might have whimpered. The door opens.

"Angel, are you in here?" Cody asks. I can see why he'd be confused. I have the lights dimmed because the bright, fluorescent lights were like taking a melon baller to my brain. I cannot help what I do next. It's a reflex my body and brain make without my thought.

"No?" I question.

"Honey, where are you?"

"No!" Rasp. "Stay back! Save yourself," I warn him. But Cody just chuckles. I hear him walk around my desk and take me in. I'm in the fetal position, crying under my desk.

"Baby, what's wrong?" He asks me sweetly.

"I'm so sick. You have to go or you'll get it too," I try again, but he just puts his palm on my brow.

"Baby, you're burning up," he tells me something I already know.

"I am a nurse, you know," I snap.

"Not a fucking smart one if you haven't been to the hospital yet," He snaps back. Well, that just burns. He's right, but still damn it!

"I'm fine. I'll be fine," I tell him.

"Yeah, after I take your ass to the hospital," he growls.

"You will do no such thing."

"I will too."

"Will not," I retort. Obviously, tiring of this volley back and forth, Cody whips out his cell phone and calls his dad, aka our boss.

"Hey, dad….Yeah….Hey, Angel is really sick, like needs to go to the hospital sick," he says into his phone. "No, not like I was away for the weekend and need to have sex with my girl, sick…Like burning up, sick….Ok. Will do. Thanks dad." He signs off from his mildly mortifying conversation with the man who signs my checks.

"Do I even want to know?" I ask, folding my arms.

"Probably not, but I'll tell you anyways. Dad says I'm to take you to the hospital and you're to let me or we're both fired. And that Gran and mom will be by this afternoon with their magical healing powers of chicken and dumplings and mint tea. And also, Steve. He's apparently a moody bastard without you and he's getting on everyone's nerves." I laugh before I can help it, but immediately start coughing.

"Okay," I say softly. "Grab my purse out of the bottom drawer, please," I ask him. Before I can say anything else, Cody is lifting me up in his arms like a bride and carrying me out to the parking lot. I feel so miserable, all I can do is lay my head on his shoulders and close my eyes. My jaw is wrenched shut so I won't give in to the coughing.

When the kids on the varsity team see us in the halls, they start singing "A Dream is a Wish Your Heart Makes" and it takes all the effort I have in me to flip those little shits off with a smile on my face. Cody throws his head back and laughs.

"She's a keeper, man," I hear Sam's deep laugh from somewhere in the hall and it makes me laugh too. Weirdo.

I think Cody is going to lead me to his old truck, but heads to my jeep and wedges my body between his and the car while her rummages through my purse for my keys.

"Jesus, this is like Mary Poppins carpet bag. What the hell all do you have in here?" He grumbles. "I half expect a magical Genie to pop out and grant me three wishes," he gripes while palming my keys. I just scowl at him until he kisses the tip of my nose.

"Ugh. Don't do that. You'll catch this plague. This infestation of death bacterias!" I yell as I try to swat him away. Cody just laughs and opens the passenger door, tucking me into the seat. He belts me in and leans my seat back a little bit with so much care, I feel like precious cargo.

Cody drives me to the hospital which is all of about 5 minutes from the school. I'm so thankful for a small town right now. I think I'm starting to feel a little loopy. Thankfully, Cody opens the door to the car for me before I can say something really embarrassing. And once again, he places my purse in my lap and carries me into the hospital.

"Hello, Hun. Long time no see," a woman greets Cody as we walk in the door. "What do we have here?"

"Hello, Ms. Marg. I have Angel."

"Angellica," I but in.

"Like I was saying, I have my girl, Angellica, here, and she is really sick with some bug she caught from the kids at school."

"Whoowhee," she says. "Must be the strep all those kids had a few weeks ago. We'll, get you in right now, doll. Go ahead and take her into room three. The doctor will be in soon. He's just checking out Mrs. Jones' new baby."

"Thank you, ma'am," he tells her before carrying me down the hall to room three.

Room three looks like any other beige room in any other medical facility that I have ever seen. Cody places me gently on the wax paper covered table and gives me a stern once over.

"Why didn't you tell me you were sick?" He asks. "Or called my mom or my Gran or your…" But he stops abruptly.

"My what?" I ask when the hair on the back of my neck rises.

"Your aunt," he says. "Why didn't you call your aunt home?"

"I'm fine," I tell him. And I am. I think.

"Damn it, Angel! You are not fine!" I flinch but he keeps on keepin on. "How do you think I would feel if something happened to you? How do you think I feel knowing you were here, suffering alone, while I was at camp?"

"It's not like I have leprosy," I say sullenly. Now, I feel like a real brat. And Cody is just standing there with his hands on his hips and his feet shoulder width apart, staring me down. Thank god, the doctor chooses that time to walk into the exam room. Jesus, is everyone in this town freaking gorgeous or what? The doctor is a little older than us. Late thirties, forty at the very most. Sandy brown hair and very familiar brown eyes. He has to be related to Sam.

"Well, what do we have here?" He asks. "I'm Dr. Wilson, but you can call me Mark." Yep, totally Sam's brother. Or hot older cousin. Young uncle? I'm mulling this thought over when Cody interrupts me.

"Apparently, nothing important because it's not leprosy," Cody fumes.

"Could we maybe act like adults?" I harp.

"You first!"

"Get out," I shout as I point to the door but fall into a huge coughing jag.

"Over my dead body," Cody counters.

"I think I can figure out what's wrong," the doctor tells me as he listens to my lungs with his stethoscope. He puts his hand on my forehead, frowning. "We need to get that temp recorded."

He puts a thermometer in my mouth. I'm still glaring at Cody. Cody is glaring at me. The doctor is checking my blood pressure. And he's doing more frowning. Finally, the thermometer beeps and the doctor takes it before I can see it.

"Stick your tongue out," he tells me and I gag on that God damned popsicle stick. I howl like a feral cal. "Nurses make the worst patients. Better the nurse, worse the patient. From what I've heard she was the best in her field in New York, you might want to wear a cup," he tells Cody. I narrow my eyes and growl.

"Truer words, my friend," Cody tells him.

"I don't think I like either of you right now," I tell them both honestly.

"Well, that's fine because here's the deal. You most definitely have bronchitis, probably strep but as you know I have to send that culture off to the labs. Your fever is 104 which you also know is very high for an adult. So, I am going to send you home with one hell of an antibiotic, some super cough meds that will probably make you sleep," He says to me and then to Cody, "But if they don't hold onto your hat because she'll be a nut."

"Now," Mark says to me, "Because of the fever and how progressed your illness is, I don't want you alone in that big rambling house. I know Mable is out of town so someone needs to stay with you," he looks pointedly at Cody.

"Not a problem, she's staying with me," he tells the doctor. "Will you go willingly?" He asks me.

"Do I have a choice?" I counter.

"You do not," he replies.

"Fine," I fold my arms akimbo

"Fine," Cody counters back.

"Is the making up worth all this drama?" The doctor asks me.

"Unfortunately, yes," I tell him through gritted teeth. Cody is standing there with a lecherous smirk on his face. "You wipe that smirk off your face or it'll be the last thing you do," I warn the jerk, waving my finger at him.

"Bet she's a hellcat," the doctor says absent mindedly.

"You have no idea," Cody tells him, smiling full out now.

Cody takes the paperwork from the nurse at the front desk. He's all about Doctors orders and prescriptions and fucking soup. My head is pounding and I kind of want to kill him. Just a little bit.

He bundles me back into my jeep and buckles me in, driving back towards the main drag where there is an old fashioned pharmacy and soda counter. I had no idea these still existed anymore, but I love it.

"I'm going to go to the counter for some tea and crackers," I tell Cody as I reach for my buckle. His hands stop my progression.

"Okay, baby. But just let me do this," I just nod. He gets out and walks around the jeep to my door and opens it, unbuckling me and pulling me out.

Cody carries me into the pharmacy and over to the soda counter. He places me on a stool and turns me around. I roll my eyes when he can't see me.

"I saw that," he tells me.

"Heard you were ill," the man at the counter tells me. I just nod because well, yeah.

"My girl would like some tea and crackers if you could." Again, I just nod. "I'll be over at the pharmacy counter," he tells me before placing a soft kiss on my forehead.

The man places my tea and crackers in front of me while I watch Cody over at the pharmacy counter hand the pharmacist my papers and then look at his watch and nod. Apparently, there will be a bit of a wait. I sip my tea and openly watch Cody grab tissues and cough drops and an arm load full of crap. The whole show makes me smile. Shit. I'm falling for Cody.

As soon as my prescriptions are ready, Cody gathers all of his take care of me crap and my meds and loads them up in the back of the jeep. Then he loads me in the jeep and drives me home. Well, not my home. His cabin.

"What do you need, baby?" He asks me softly.

"A shower? Maybe? I feel gross," I tell him.

"I can do you one better," he tells me as he carries me up the stairs with my head on his shoulder.

Cody walks right through his bedroom and into the bathroom, but instead of the shower, Cody turns on the big soaker tub in the corner and checks the temperature. Carefully, he removes my clothes piece by piece as he stands in front of me and then slowly lowers my body into the warm water.

I lean my head back as Cody lovingly washes my hair. It's not the first time he's done this, but it is the first time where I needed him to care for me with no hanky panky before or after. He takes a washcloth in hand and lathers it up with soap and gently washes the icky feeling from my body.

Once I'm all cleaned up, he pulls the plug from the drain in the old tub, and towels off my body. He places one of his t-shirts over my head and grabs a pair of his cotton sweat pants. The kind with the elastic waist and ankles and pulls them up my legs. They're huge, but they make me feel comfy and smell like Cody, so I'm happy. He slips on a pair of his white gym socks over my feet and then carefully carries me over to the bed where he pulls back the covers and tucks me in. As soon as the blankets are pulled up over my body, Steve is barreling up the stairs and in the bed.

"I'll go talk to mom for a bit and then I'll be back to check on you," he says as he kisses my nose again. "You're on duty, Steve," he tells my companion. Steve just drapes his big furry head over my waist and closes his eye on a sigh. I smile at Cody before closing my eyes too, as I absently run my fingers through the fur in between Steve's ears. Before I know it, I'm off to sleep.

Cody

It's been three days and I still cannot believe how sick Angel was when I found her in her office. I'm still pretty damn livid when I think about how she didn't call anyone. She didn't call me and she didn't call Mable. I know her mom is dead, but her dad is right here in town and she doesn't even know. Or he's such an angry asshole that he didn't even check on her while she was ill. I'm pissed at her and I'm pissed at him. I'm irrationally pissed at me for being away at camp. I'm feeling a little crazy and a little on edge lately, so I went for a run.

The first two days, I didn't leave her side. Or at the very least the house. But I'm so wound up, I need the release. Other releases have also been off the table and my dick does not understand what my brain is telling him. We're at a stalemate.

I'm running up the steps of the house, Steve matching me step for step. I open the front door and there is movement in the lower part of the house. Life in the house again. I missed it. Angel had me worried.

Steve and I follow the noise into the kitchen where my dick and I are both stopped in our tracks. Because dancing around the kitchen is my Angel and she's wearing nothing but my t-shirt. The sight does things to me. Good things. Territorial things. And a warm feeling seers across my chest.

I must have made a noise because Angel is looking up at me and smiling. I walk over to her as if I never had a choice. I don't. I'm drawn to her. To her light. I brush her unruly hair back from her face and kiss her temple as I wrap my arms around her. She leans into the kiss, into my embrace and damn if that doesn't feel good too.

"How are you feeling, baby?" I ask her and her smile brightens even more.

"Great. Still a little tired, but great," she tells me. "The sheets are in the washer and I was just about to have a yogurt."

"You didn't have to do that," I tell her. Getting her one of those God awful yogurts that's barely yogurt because it's covered in candy out of the fridge and hand it to her with a spoon.

"Thanks, babe," she says softly. She looks a little flustered by the look on my face, which I hope doesn't show how much I've missed her. How much I want her. But then she drops her spoon to the floor and when she bends over to pick it up, I groan because the sight is exactly what I want. She stalks closer to me, swinging her lush hips.

"Wh-what are you doing?" I ask her. She just smirks.

"You, lover," she tells me before she drops to her knees in front of me and unties the string on my running shorts. Before I can form any coherent thoughts, she has my cock in her hand and is stroking me. A gurgle noise comes out of my mouth.

"Angel..." I rasp as she swirls the tip in her mouth and then plunges my cock all the way in. I suck in a deep breath as she bobs up and down on my cock. My hands find their way into her hair and I grip it. Hard. She gets one more good rotation in before I pull her off of me, my shirt off her body, I toss her onto her back on the counter top of the big island in the kitchen.

"Cody…" She says on a whoosh of an exhale when I latch my mouth over her center. I kiss her deeply between her thighs and feel her start to shake. I push two finger into her core and she's soaked. My Angel is needy. "Cody…." She says again. She's close, but she started this hot and fast and that's exactly what it's going to be.

I pull my fingers from her body and she lets out the soft mewl that drives me wild and spread her legs wide, wider than they can go as I stand up. I thrust my cock deep all at once and we both suck in a breath.

"You played with fire, Angel," I tell her as I pull out and thrust hard and deep. I lean over her caging her in with my body.

"Yes," she tells me, clawing at my back.

"Are you going to do it again?" I ask her.

"Yes," she breathes.

"Thank God," I tell her as I take us both over the edge.

When we both catch our breath, I kissed her sweetly. God, I think I could love this woman. I never thought I would want to be back here again, but here I am. I smile against her neck, nipping as I stand up and pull from her body. The look on Angel's face probably mirrors my own displeasure at being separated from her.

I smirk as I pull my shorts back up, having never really taken them off. It appears my girl missed me as much as I missed her while she was recuperating. I need to remind myself she's still recovering from a bad bout. I reach my hand out to her and she takes it, letting me help her from the counter.

Hand in hand we walk through the kitchen and up the stairs, her heart pounding like mine is, I'm sure. Neither one of us speaking. When we make it to the bedroom, our bedroom, damn if that doesn't sound good too, I lead her right to the shower.

I kiss her beautiful body as I silently wash away the evidence of our hurried moment in the warm shower spray. Her skin is flushing pink with her need. I should say no, but I can't. I can never say no to her, so, when she reaches for me, I kiss her soundly as she strokes me. I back her into the shower wall. I run my hands down her back, and over her thigh, squeezing it before I push it up to wrap around my back. She has to let go of my cock when I grip her ass in my palms and lift her up. Angel instinctually wraps her arms around my neck and presses her other leg to match the first, as I grind against her center.

I kiss all over her face, her lips, her eyes, her cheeks, pulling back so she has to see my face, read every emotion on it as I slip my body into hers. Unlike the first time we were together in this shower, we are unhurried. I slowly rock into her as we stare into each other's eyes. This moment is changing everything. I can feel it. I know Angel feels it too.

I feel her body grip me tighter and hear the soft gasp as she gets closer and closer to her release. I pick up my pace but continue the gentle rocking in and out of her body, nothing is rushed or hurried, and everything is soft and….loving.

I kiss Angel's lips again and make my way to her jaw and down the side of her neck to that spot that makes her wild. I continue my path down to her shoulder as I rock faster and faster into her. Her breath coming shorter and faster, her chest rising and falling. She is starting to come apart in my arms, and I love it. I'm so close too. The only thing missing are the words. We have yet to say the words. I can't hold back any longer. I bite down on her shoulder to keep the words in as I push into her body deep, one last time as I come. That was all my Angel needed as she followed me over the edge.

I decided Angel and I need some time out of the house in public places where there was no privacy, or beds and showers, or any hard surface I could take her on or up against. The need to make Angel see how much I have come to love her is clawing at my insides. And yet, I can't bring myself to say the words.

So, I've decided we'll go to the diner for lunch and I'll tell her there. This plan is twofold. One, I need to nut up and tell her I love her. Two, I feel like if I say it while my dick is deep, and I mean deep, she won't believe the sentiment is genuine.

So, here we are sitting at the table gazing lovingly into each other's eyes over club sandwiches and malts. This is it. This is my moment. I'm going to tell the greatest girl in the world how I have fallen in love with her. Oh, shit. I sound like such a tool. I think I have heartburn. I feel like I'm going to throw up or shit my pants all at the same time. That can't be good.

I excuse myself to the bathroom so I can splash water on my face. I'm leaning over the sink deciding whether or not I'm going to hurl when Sam walks in. He has a disgusted look on his face.

"Are you going to grow a set or what?" He asks me.

"I have no idea what you're talking about," I feign innocence.

"You are going to lose that girl if you don't get your shit for brains ass out there and claim her as yours once and for all," he thunders. I open my mouth to speak but can't find the words. "Take it from someone who has seen it happen. Life is unpredictable, and sometimes cut unfairly short. Make sure when your ticket gets punched that you have no regrets on your conscious." And with that Sam claps me twice on the back and leaves.

After Sam's girlie powwow in the bathroom, I am more than ready. He's right, I love Angel. I am going to tell her and I'm going to keep her. Maybe marry her. Have lots of football loving babies and lots more sex. I walk out of the restroom, ready to claim my girl, and instead life kicks me in the nuts. Again. Jesus, can I get a break?

TWELVE

Angellica

Oh, fuck. That's all I can think in my head. Is this shit really even happening? Dear, God, it's me Angellica, what the fuck? Okay? How can one person's luck seriously be this bad? I can't figure it out. And trust me I'm trying.

Imagine my surprise when I'm off having a good day with my man that I finally feel better. I can surprise my man with some post run surprises of the naked variety. Only to to find him surprising me by really making love to me in the shower. He might not have said the words, but I saw them. I felt them. Fuck, now I sound crazy. I wonder if any of those meds I'm on have any lasting side effects or ramifications. Like insanity.

Then Cody hustles us off to lunch at the diner and we're having a really great time. Sure, sometimes he makes a face that says he might be suffering from dysentery, but that's ok. I'm a nurse. I can pop an IV line with fluids in my sleep. But he holds my hand and talks to me. He laughs with me. So I think we're all good.

That is until he goes to the restroom. And he's in there for a really long freaking time. He might really have dysentery. Or at the very least a case of ptomaine poisoning. I saw some highly questionable things in his refrigerator this morning while I looking for something to eat before I gnawed my own arm off. Seriously! I am not one of those girls that can survive on half a side salad with no dressing. Jesus, eat a cheeseburger. I'm just glad Cody didn't come home sooner. I had already had a power bar, two slim jims, why Mr. I-only-eat-healthy has them in his pantry I don't know, I didn't ask, I just ate them. And a block of cheese. The yogurt was a chaser. I'm a bad eater, I will admit, but not that bad. After three days of soup broth and tea, my body went into survival mode and it was about to get real.

So, Cody is in the restroom for a curious amount of time and I'm sitting at our table waiting for him, thinking about how great my life is right now. You know, rule number one of things you should never do! And then BAM! Jackass Joe sits down across from me in the booth where Cody just was sitting.

"To what do we owe the displeasure of your visit, doctor?" I ask in my best artificial sweet voice.

"Don't you think this town is beneath you?" He asks back, bored.

"No," I reply honestly.

"Come now, stop playing games," he says as if he has a right to be mad. I just sit back and fold my arms over my chest, shaking my head no.

"I'm not playing games," I say honestly. "I'm really happy here."

"Don't lie to me," he says with a smug smile playing on his cruel mouth. "I know you miss me. You can't possibly have our chemistry with anyone else." I'm just about to ask him what chemistry if he was banging Nurse Erin, when a big strong body slides into the bench seat next to me and wraps me in his arms.

Cody kisses me like his life depends on it and I swear my toes curl. I grab the front of his t-shirt in my hands and pull him closer to me. Kissing him back. Deeply. There are a few good natured whistles and cat calls around the diner before he releases me.

"She has found great chemistry," Cody says to Joe with that winning smirk on his face. "With me," he smiles with his arm around my shoulder and my body pulled tight to his side.

"You're dating someone? Already?" Joe asks as if I'm the one in the wrong.

"Joe, you were already sleeping with someone else. Before we broke up," I reminded him.

"That doesn't count and you know it!" Umm what?

"Uhh, yeah it does."

"Now, you listen here and you listen good, you little brat," Joe narrows his eyes on me and leans forward. "I am the best doctor in New York. You do not get to embarrass me. If I say we are not breaking up, we're not fucking breaking up. And if I say you will get your fat ass on the six o'clock plane to New York, your ass is on the fucking plane. Get it?" He's shouting. And actually I don't get it, so I narrow my eyes back at him, but Cody just laughs. I mean really laughs. This cannot be good.

"Look, man, I get it. It burns your pride," Cody tells Joe in his sexy southern drawl. I never noticed it so much before until it was laid next to Joe's voice. "But I don't much take too kindly to people threatening my fiancée." He drops the bomb. Uhh, what did he just say? I hear gasps go up throughout the diner.

"You cannot be serious."

"As a heart attack, mister," Cody says back. "We were just out celebrating. Fixing to go give my mama and Ms. Mable the good news."

"Oh, God! Mable's here?" Joe asks scooting lower in his seat. And if I'm not mistaken, Cody sits just a little taller. "That crazy old bat has had it out for me for forever. The first thing I'll do when we're married is lock her away in a home," he smirks at me.

"You will do no such thing, you son of a bitch!" I scream at him as I lunge across the table. "Mable is only fifty four you tool!"

"Now, now, darlin'," Cody says sweetly as he tightens his grip on my body pulling me back across the table into the safe zone. "If you get arrested for assault we can't go give Mable the good news."

"You're right, baby, I just got a little carried away in the moment," I smile at him.

"Well, I know all about how you can get swept away in a moment," he says as he gives me a look that's meant to tell everyone he's seen me naked and liked it. I feel my cheeks heat and I look away, smiling. "But let's just make it the right kind of moment," he winks at me. Joe narrows his eyes on us again.

"If you're really engaged, why don't you have a ring?" He asks looking like the cat that just caught the canary.

"Oh, that's easy. It's in the safe at my mama and daddy's place, just up around the bend from ours," Cody says.

"But you didn't give it to her when you proposed?" Joe asks trying to catch us in our lies.

"Well, I'd tell you how I proposed, but it was when we were both over swept by a moment and not fit to share," Cody says with a smile and a look at me. My whole face has to be bright red.

"This is beneath you," he looks pointedly at me. I just shrug. "Fine. Prove to me that you're engaged. I guess I'll be staying here for a while," he challenges. Oh, shit.

So we do what any normal people caught in important lies do, we lie some more and hope we don't get caught. So, Cody pays for our lunch and walks me to the jeep. Jackass climbs in the front passenger seat before I can and I am reminded of some of the things that drive me nuts. Like his always taking the better seat everywhere. The better meal choice. The better side of the bed. What the fuck? Cody looks annoyed but just shakes his head.

He climbs in the driver's seat and leads us home, to hopefully find some kind of a ring before we get caught in this shit show. At least we've been staying together for a while so it's not going to be awkward when we fake close quarters interactions.

We reach the big gate of the ranch and pass through the arch way that I have come to love. Cody pulls the jeep in front of his parent's big farm house on the left. Before Cody even opens his door, his mama is opening the front door and stepping out onto the big, white porch. Steve is bolting out of the house and jumping on me. Joe makes a disgusted noise in the back of his throat.

"Hey, buddy. Did you miss me?" I ask him as his tail wags back and forth. "Oh, my good boy. I always miss you. I wonder if I could take you to school with me."

"Hey, baby," Mrs. Reynolds says to Cody. "What brings y'all by?" She asks but she winks at him. That sly fox knows. I don't know how but she knows.

"Well, mama, Angel and I are getting married," he tells his mom with a proud smile on his face. She pauses two point five seconds before she gives the best excited squeal ever and jumps up and down wrapping her arms around Cody and giving him a huge hug.

I can't help but be a little jealous that I will never have a moment like that with my mom, even if she was still alive. She would have hated that I settled here and loved to see me married to a rich asshole like Joe. Mrs. Reynolds walks down the porch steps and wraps her strong arms around me in a real hug and whispers in my ear the words I have always wanted to hear, even if they are fake.

"You are the daughter I have always wanted. I could not be more excited that you are joining our family. Ooooohhh, and won't your babies be pretty!" She jumps up and down, clapping.

"Let's not get ahead of ourselves here," I tell her, but Cody is nodding in full agreement, traitor!

"I agree. Babies. Lots and lots of babies," he smiles at me. "I can't wait to see you with a big round belly and my baby in it." And I almost believe him.

"Well, let's go get your ring!" Mrs. Reynolds claps. "Now, I was thinking of a little something different," she tells us as she leads us all into the dining room where there are little velvet boxes lined up on the table.

"Is that what I think it is, mama?" Cody asks softly and I can swear there are tears in his eyes that he is holding back. They match his mother's as she answers.

"If you mean the Williams ring, then yes it is," she says softly.

"Mama," Cody whispers.

"You could use that ugly little thing you got, but our Angel is the next woman to wear the Williams ring. It chose her. I swear it. I opened the safe and it fell on my head. If that's not a sign, then I don't give a hoot what is," she declares.

"I couldn't agree more," Cody says as he gives his mom a hug and a kiss on the cheek. Then he slowly grabs the black velvet box in his hand and closes his eyes as he tips his head ever so slightly forward in thought.

"Cody?" I ask. But he gently grabs my left hand as he drops to one knee and says the words I wish with all my heart he was saying to me for real.

"Angellica Andrews, I come to you a humble man who is madly, desperately in love with you. You have woven yourself into my life so strongly, I cannot imagine the rest of my life without you. You are so amazing, so smart, so beautiful, great ass, and so, so loving. Please, say you'll marry me and let me give you babies and a long, beautiful life."

"Yes," I say, with tears streaming down my face. Because I'm a decent enough person, but who says no to all of their hopes and dreams in one perfect package. I'm strong but not that strong. So it's with tears and laughter, and not just mine, Cody puts a large diamond on my finger and kisses the hell out of me.

"What the hell is a Williams ring besides a big piece of glass?" Joe barks, breaking us all free from the magic spell we've woven.

"The Williams ring is an engagement ring that was commissioned by my grandfather for my grandmother in 1900," Mrs. Reynolds explains calmly with narrowed eyes. "It is a nine carat oval diamond surrounded by another carats worth of smaller diamonds including a delicate leaf pattern on each side that leads into the band."

"Are you sure you want me to wear this ring? It's so special. And Valuable," I ask.

"Yeah," Cody says softly.

"The Williams ring was left in trust to my mother and me for Cody. It was always intended that he have this ring to give to his wife. That is as long as we were sure she was worthy. And you are so worth it. Take care of my boy," she tells me. I just nod. "Well, then. I suppose you'll be off to show Mable. Bring her back here for supper and we'll all celebrate with a big dinner at the main house." She claps her hands and dismisses us.

So we all pile back in my jeep. Cody growling a little when Joe shoves me in the backseat of my own car. They keep shooting side eyes at each other. Me, on the other hand, am wondering what the fuck just happened as I sit and stare at the giant fucking ring on my finger. I feel eyes on my face so I look up and catch Cody's golden gaze in the rear view mirror. He winks at me and I give him the best smile I can muster. I am so fucked.

THIRTEEN

Cody

Thank fuck the drive from my parents' place to Ms. Mable's is all of about ten minutes on a bad day because I keep vacillating back and forth between thinking this Joe character is a huge douche bag and watching Angel in the rear view mirror look at my great-grandmother's engagement ring with wonder and hope in her eyes.

And if that doesn't make a man feel good to see his girl fall in love with his grandmother's ring. Angel is the first girl I have ever been serious about that really fit, clicked with my family, with my town, my life. Hell, even my dog. My parents love her. Like really love her. She makes my Gran laugh and laughs at the crazy shit my Gran says back. And these are the thoughts I can't stop from running through my brain while I drive this circus back to town.

I should have known my mother would call Mable and give her the skinny on this fake engagement bullshit. When I pulled the jeep to a stop, Mable ran down the porch stairs, and down the walk, throwing her arms around Angel so hard she had to take a step back to keep her aunt from taking her to the ground. It was a good move. I was proud.

"My sweet girl! I'm so happy for you," she tells Angel with her palms on either of her cheeks. She takes her niece's left hand in hers with tears in her eyes as she looks at the ring. "I'm so, so happy. Now, how about those babies?" She asks and I just laugh. Sounds like a good idea to me. A brief thought flits through my brain, that I know where Angel keeps her birth control pills in the bathroom drawer, and I should just flush them down the toilet, but that would probably piss her off.

I take a good look at Angel. She's still not one hundred percent, so she's in these weird jean legging super hybrid pants she seems to fancy, and they make her ass look fantastic, so I have no complaints. A light pink and a white ribbed tank tops one over the other skim over and hint at her beautiful body. She's got these little black shoes on her feet that look like slippers. They're kind of ridiculous but she's so cute I can't help but smile. There is no makeup on her face, and honestly, she doesn't need it. Her blue eyes are bright and her cheeks pink with excitement. I love seeing it. The best part is, she's left those wild blonde curls down. I just want to grab them and wrap the springy coils around my fingers. Yep, I got it bad. But Sam was right. I'm ok with it. Let's see where this adventure takes us.

"Do you need to grab a dress for tonight from your closet here, or do you have something at the house you can wear to dinner?" Mable asks Angel.

"I didn't realize we were dressing for dinner," she tells her grandmother.

"Oh yes, Cody's grandmother is putting together a lovely dinner party in your honor, sweethearts. You'll love it. And she really knows how to do it up."

"This is true," I tell her.

"I have that silk dress I wore to church a few weeks ago…." But everyone is making a face at me.

"What about that white flowy dress?" Aunt Mable suggests.

"Is that the low cut one?" Cody asks. He knows which dress it is. I've only worn it once when we went out to dinner.

"You know it is," I tell him giving him my best school nurse glare.

"Wear that one but with no underwear," he tells me and I just roll my eyes. I should have gone for my ER nurse glare. Clearly, I'm losing my touch.

"I am most definitely wearing panties to your grandmother's dinner party," I tell him, but he's giving me big sad puppy dog eyes.

"She always was a spoilsport," Aunt Mable tells him. "She gets that from her mother."

"You two are incorrigible," I tell them both, shaking my head but smiling at them as I do it.

After Aunt Mable rushed upstairs to throw on a gorgeous soft pink, pleated, sleeveless silk dress that tied in a bow at a modest but sexy vee, and with a hem came to her knees. She paired it with a beige, braided leather belt and matching pumps. Mable is still gorgeous. Still turning heads. Her blonde curls are smoothed into a 1940s wave that only she can pull off. Paired with soft pink makeup, she looks very mother of the bride. It stings my heart to think it, but if I was really getting married, I would want Mable to give me away.

Mable is the only parent I really ever had. My mother travelling all around the world with her rich husband was never there, and who in the hell even knew who my father was. He sure enough hasn't shown his face in my life in the last twenty five years.

We all pile back in the jeep and again, Joe takes the front. Mable narrows her eyes on the back of his head, Cody just shakes his head, as if he'd said Joe is such a moron, and I just shrug when they look at me. He's not my problem anymore.

The short drive back to The Reynold's ranch is tense and done silently. Each of us lost in our own thoughts. When Cody pulls the jeep up in front of his cabin we all hop out and head for the front porch.

"Y'all go on upstairs and hurry up. I'll get the good doctor something to drink," Aunt Mable says on an eye roll. I am seriously hoping this drink doesn't include arsenic or rat poison.

Cody and I take off up the stairs. He's headed straight for the shower and I head for my makeup and hair stuff to get this mess looking decent. Before I make it a foot away from him, Cody is swinging me up into his arms and I shriek.

"What are you doing?" I ask a little breathless, seeing him shirtless.

"Join me in the shower?" He asks with that sexy smile on his face. I think about it. If I pin my hair up now, it'll probably be ok and if it's not I'll just put it up in a bun. It would work with that dress. So I offer him up my sassy smile.

"Okay," And before I have even finished saying that one little word, my top is off, my bra is flying. "Hey. I'll need that later!" I shout but he doesn't care. He is pulling my jeans and panties down my legs and his fingers are taking some serious detours.

Cody picks me up again in a fireman hold over his shoulder and drops his own jeans and underpants as he walks us both into the shower. I can't help the laughter that comes out with his playful side. When he hears me and all my laughter, he swats my butt. Hard. My laughter is cut off as he walks us into the warm spray.

He slowly slides my body back down his and I take a step back when I see the look in his eyes. It's...intense. But he's right there crowding me in. His palms against the shower wall on either side of my head. I get one more look at him before he kisses me. Hard. Before sliding one of his hands down my body, over my belly. I can't help the shiver that racks my body when his hands trail between my legs. I know Cody feels it because he smirks at me.

"We don't have a lot of time," I tell him.

"Then we'll just have to be fast," he answers as he turns me around so I'm facing the wall. Cody glides his palms up my spine and then down each of my arms, one by one lifting my hands so they brace me against the stone shower wall, running his thumb over the ring on my left hand.

Cody skims his nose down my neck, behind my ear. Nipping as he goes. He takes my hips in his Strong hands and gently tips them back. I have a second to prepare before he plunges in deep. I call out. His strokes are hard and fast. His hands will no doubt leave bruises on my hips and I love it.

There is nothing sweet or gentle about what is happening here. But that doesn't make it any less amazing. Or hot. But it dawns on me that Cody is marking his territory following the sudden appearance of my crappy ex-boyfriend demanding I follow him home.

My fingernails are not finding purchase on the stone wall as I try to find something to grab on to. Not that it matters. I'm already gone. We fall to the shower floor as I lose my grip but Cody never separates from me. We land with me cradled in his arms, his knees taking the brunt of the fall. My ass the rest. As we settle on the ground, me balanced on my ass, my shoulders held off the tile floor by Cody's strong arms, Cody balanced on his knees with one palm on the floor for support. He manages to bring his thrusts to a crescendo. Harder and faster. Both of us there. I feel the sting as the power of Cody's movements scrapes my ass against the tile floor but it does not stop me. I call out again as I come. Cody shouts my name as he comes with me.

We lay there for a minute lost in each other's arms as we catch our breath. When our hearts slow down, he kisses me long and sweet on the mouth before pulling from my body and standing up. He reaches a hand out to help me up off the ground and I take it.

"There's no other woman like you, Angel," he says as he kisses the tip of my nose and then quickly washes both of our bodies.

By the time we dry off and step out of the shower, we need to hustle. Cody runs to the closet and throws on a navy blue suit, black dress shoes and socks, and a white dress shirt, no tie, opened at the collar. Holy, shit he's hot. I gawk as I watch him in the bathroom mirror.

I run the opposite way to the bathroom and quickly pin my unruly curls up in a bun on top of my head. I'm doing my makeup in the mirror when I notice him behind me. I have my foundation and powder on already and I'm using a big fluffy brush to apply my pink blush to my cheeks.

"What?" I ask. But he doesn't answer me.

"Mable, you still here?" He shouts down the stairs. When he is greeted with no answer back from either Aunt Mable or Joe, he looks at me again. "We're going to be a little late."

"No, we're already late."

"Okay, we're going to be more late," I give him my best stern look but he just carries on. "You should of thought about consequences before you stood there gloriously naked, bent over my bathroom counter doing what you're doing."

"It's just makeup," I shout.

"It might be, but it's really you naked, bent over my bathroom counter," he tells me. I turn around and look at him. Really look at him. His hazel eyes are glowing as he looks at me. His suit is perfect for his body, in fact, I'd bet it was custom made it fits him so well. As I continue to take stock of how handsome he is I notice the front if his slacks is appearing to have some problems.

"Well, I guess the day a man gets engaged, real or fake, is an important one," I say as I skim my fingers down the row of buttons on his shirt, stopping only at his belt to unbuckle it.

"That, it is. That it is," his retort is husky.

I unhook his pants and slowly lower the zipper, tucking my fingers into the waistband as I push his slacks and boxers down to his knees. His erection springs free. I scrape my nails down his thighs as I lower myself to my knees. I take him in my hand and slowly stroke him before leaning forward to take him in my mouth. Cody runs his fingertips over my jaw and I look up and into his eyes as I take him all the way into my mouth. I decide then that this will be the best blow job of my life. Hollowing my cheeks, I move up and down his cock. He leans forward, gripping the edge of the countertop behind me.

I don't let up on him. And before I know it he's growing in my mouth. He tries to pull back, but I grab on to his hips with my hands and pull his body closer to me, his cock deeper in my mouth. He growls as he comes down my throat.

I stand back up and pretending like that didn't just happen, finish putting on my makeup with a little nude shimmery eye shadow and black mascara. My lips need no lipstick as they are swollen and pink, so I add a little clear gloss that's cherry flavored.

Cody is still standing there, gripping the counter around me, his cock still hang out of his pants. I just wink at him in the mirror, ducking under his arm I saunter to the closet, swinging my hips as I go knowing he's watching and the look on his face promises retribution. Yipee!

When we walked into Cody's grandparents' house everyone was already there and imbibing in the free flowing cocktails. I did not feel this boded well for the situation. The assembled crowd which included an angry looking Aunt Mable, both sets of Cody's grandparents, his parents, a sour faced Joe, Sam and his wife, Holt, and the Mayor. Which I thought was weird. He looked to be his usual cranky self. Yay! How fun.

We were all called to dinner and sat around the long dining room table. Cody's grandfather at one end, his grandmother next to him. Aunt Mable fought the Mayor for the other end of the table and won, he still sat next to her. Cody's parents sat next to him and that left me to sit in between Joe and Cody. Fuck my life. Do you even wonder how you end up in certain situations? Well, lately, that's every damn day of my life.

"Do you have any idea of what kind of a wedding you would like, dear?" Mrs. Reynolds asks me.

"I'm not sure yet. It all happened so suddenly," I smile at her.

"Do you think you'd like to have the wedding here at the ranch?" His grandmother asks me hopefully.

"That sounds lovely!" Mable chimes in. I look to Cody for help but he just smiles indulgently at me.

"Angel can have whatever she wants. I'm just happy to be the man she'll be meeting at the alter," he says over the soup course. Deserter! Things went a little sideways over the prime rib and twice baked potatoes when the conversation turned to when.

"I think you'd make a lovely June bride," Mable says sweetly. I coughed on my delicious prime rib.

"That's a splendid idea! I think us ladies could put a wedding together for the beginning of June," Mrs. Reynolds claps. "What do you say ladies?!" Which was met with raucous cheers from Cody's grandmothers and Mable.

"Don't you think this is all a bit sudden?" The Mayor snaps.

"I'm not sure how this decision concerns you," Mable narrows her eyes at him and I can't help but squirm. I see Cody flinch out of the corner of my eye, but he covers it well.

"That's unfair and you know it," he says softly. I feel a tingle along the back of my neck but don't have time to put any thought in it because Joe chooses that moment to pipe up.

"I think the Mayor is correct. This is too sudden. You're not thinking clearly, Angie. You've obviously been brain washed by this…this…sex fiend!" He shouts. I cringe and try and slither under the table but Cody stops my progress. One look at him confirms he's smiling like a loon. Bastard.

"I don't know what you're talking about," I hedge, hoping Joe will realize his faux pas, but he just keeps getting more and more angry.

"I fucking heard you," he thunders. While I was sitting in the kitchen with your nut bag aunt."

"This is true. I was pretty impressed," Aunt Mable tells the table at the same time the Mayor shouts at Joe.

"Who are you to call anyone a nut bag? Actually, who the hell are you anyways?" He asks. "Actually, I don't care. But if I ever hear you make threats or unsavory comment to Mable ever again, I will call the sheriff and have your ass thrown in jail." The room was quiet for a bit until Holt chimes in.

"I'm the sheriff and things have been a little slow lately. I'd do it just for entertainment value," Holt says honestly. I'm so stunned at the crazy turns this evening is taking that I'm shoveling in my dinner hoping no one will direct the conversation back to me. Unfortunately, my luck is still a flaming pile of Steve's crap.

"You should slow down on the potatoes, Angie. Actually, you shouldn't eat them at all if you ever want to shed some of that fat," Joe says to me. And you could hear a pin drop.

"I think it's time for you to go," Holt says quietly, but firmly. "If you're nice I'll drive you to the airport. If you continue to be a jackass, I'll take you straight to jail." Joe just stands, dropping his napkin on his plate and follows Holt out the door. We all sat there in silence for a few minutes before I turned to Cody, not quite meeting his eyes.

"I'd like to go now," I say softly, humiliated.

"Nonsense!" Principal Reynolds booms. "What you need is tequila," which magically manifests in front of me. I immediately shoot it back and Cody's grandfather fills my glass back up. I shoot that back too.

"I think I'm ok now," I rasp as the booze sears across my chest.

"Not yet but you will be soon. What an asshole. Let's get the cake, love. We'll all feel better with cake," his grandfather says. I'm not so sure. I'm feeling a little green around the gills.

"Definitely. What her ass needs is cake. What a moron. I would feed an ass like that every day," Cody's dad says as his wife slaps his chest. "What? It's a fantastic ass. Mark my words, son, don't let her lose that ass." My face is beet red and I will never be able to look anyone in the eye ever again. I feel Cody's body shake with laughter next to me.

"I won't dad. In fact, I had that very thought the first time Angel joined Holt, Sam, and me for pizza at Father's," he tells the table. I just throw my head back and laugh because every word he spoke rings absolutely true.

Angellica

Taylor Swift's "Out of the Woods" is blaring in my ears. Oh, fuck. My head is pounding in time to the alarm clock on Cody's night stand. It's not his alarm clock. It's mine. The beautiful fucker is a morning person. So he's off running and frolicking through the woods while I'm here trying to swallow a bag of cotton balls. Well, that's at least what it feels like.

I shut the alarm off and head to the bathroom to brush out the taste of where tequila died in my mouth. The feel of the bristles of my toothbrush on my tongue makes me yark. So I brush again. This time, giving myself the hairy eyeball in the mirror. Throw up and die, bitch.

The shower is next. I'm pretty sure the tequila Cody's grandad kept filling me with last night is seeping out of my pores. It's not a good feeling. So, I throw up in the shower too, just for good measure. I'm standing in the shower under the spray. Just standing there looking at my toes. This is how Cody finds me.

"Babe!" He shouts at me. I can't help the wince. There is a conga line in my head. Cody jumps in the shower fully clothed. "Babe, they want to induct me into the Hall of Fame in New York," he's so excited and I love seeing it.

"That's wonderful," I say in a whisper. I give him the best smile I can. But I'm pretty sure it's a grimace.

"Hangover?" He asks me with a smirk on his face. When I narrow my eyes he adds, "Amateur. Gramps and Tequila go back to his Army days. You should never drink with him unless you're prepared for the consequences."

"I do not like this lecture. Get out or die," I growl. He just laughs. Crazy bastard.

I continue to soap up, wash my hair. I lean my face into the spray when I feel something poke me from behind. Nope. Not today, no sir. I finish washing the cleanser off my face and then step out of the shower and towel off.

"You wound me, love!" Cody calls from within the shower.

"You'll survive," I shout back. Wincing at the volume. "My head will not," he just chuckles.

I make my way into the closet and slip on plain cotton pant-ies and a cotton bra. I'm not feeling very fancy today. But it's Texas and late spring early summer so it's hot out. I button up a white sleeveless shirt that has pockets over the boobies and slip in my favorite red, pleated silk skirt with little blue and white flowers all over it. I add a tan leather braided belt and tan leather ballet flats.

By the time I'm done tying my curls up in a messy bun and applying a light amount of makeup, Cody had beat me down stairs. Granted he wears workout clothes to school. He was in the kitchen laying scrambled eggs, bacon, and toast on plates at the island and pouring cups of coffee to go with. God, I love this man. Where my stomach was previously sour, the smell of the eggs and toast got me. I picked up a toast square and delicately nibble the edges. Okay, this is okay. I sipped some black coffee to burn the rest of the booze out of my gut and then hesitantly picked up my fork. After two or three bites, I was suddenly ravenous and before I knew it, my breakfast was gone. Huh, how did that happen? So I reached over and took two more bites of Cody's eggs before sticking my plate in the sink to rinse. Cody just laughed.

We loaded the breakfast dishes in the dishwasher and headed to school together. He drove me to work in my jeep and in the parking lot we parted ways with a quick promise to meet for lunch. I was feeling so much better by the time I got to my office. But still, I'm never drinking again.

There's only a couple of days left before graduation and school lets out for the summer. I'm only here to make sure no one breaks their arm or worse on slip n slides on the field or faking sick so they won't have to take their finals. The answer is no you're not dying of the plague. And yes, you do have to take your finals.

A couple hours into the day, but still a ways off from lunch, Cody pops his head through my door. I'm a little surprised to see him because he said he wouldn't be by until noon. He smiles at me and I can't help but smile back. He brightens my day.

"You alone?" He asks me.

"Yeah," I look at him with a question in my eyes. But he just walks in and shuts the door behind him, turning the lock.

Cody slowly paces towards me with a certain twinkle in his eye that I'm not sure means I should be excited or I should head for the hills. He stops in front of where I'm sitting in my chair and holds a hand out to me. I take it and slowly rise from my chair. Still not sure what's going on here.

"I missed you," he tells me.

"I missed you too," I smile at him.

He slowly walks me backwards towards my exam tables. He keeps gently pushing me back. Rubbing his hands up and down my arms. When my butt hits the back of the table, he slowly slides my body up to sit on it, his hands gripping my hips and his eyes never leaving mine.

"But today, you put this skirt on to punish me."

"I did no such thing," I say sternly as he pushes my skirt up my thighs, nodding seriously.

"You did and that's not very nice. So now, I can't wait for lunch time," he tells me as he slides my plain panties down my legs, pocketing them. Dirty bastard.

"Okay," I breathe as he slowly presses my knees open and leans in between. His fingers dig into my naked hips as he licks me. Slowly at first but quickly he picks up speed. Nipping and kissing as he goes. My legs are shaking, trying to close on their own but he mercilessly holds them open. I grab onto his hair and rock against him, biting my lip to keep from crying out, I come. He wipes his mouth along my inner thigh and rolls my skirt back down. I'm still trying to catch my breath when he leans over me and whispers.

"Now we're even for last night," and he winks at me.

"Okay," is all I can manage. I'm so damn witty and sharp. No wonder all the boys are beating down my door.

"I have one more meeting this morning before lunch. Do you have more work to do?" He asks me.

"Oh, yeah. I have more parents to call and tell them they forgot to get their kid a tetanus shot and need to do so before training for fall sports picks up," I tell him.

"Ok. But I want to talk to you about New York," He tells me. "So, come and get me when you're done. Say about an hour?"

"Okay?" I guess. "I'll meet you in an hour. But what about New York?" I ask.

"Come with me?" He smiles like a little boy as he asks me. I nod. My heart pangs for a little boy with sandy brown hair and golden hazel eyes. A little boy that steals my heat every day by giving me his dad's goofy, crooked smile. Too bad that's just a dream.

It's just past forty minutes since Cody left me with promises of New York and his Hall of Fame induction. That's a big deal. I would need a nice dress and I would probably throw up being judged by all those people. But I'm so excited. I can show him all the places I loved growing up. I am practically skipping down the hall to the sports offices. But just outside the door, I hear heated words being exchanged.

"Do you really think you should marry her?" The Mayor asks.

"I really think it's none of your business," Cody shoots back.

"I get it," he placates. "It was fake yesterday, but that jackass is gone now. Why does she still have a ring on her finger?"

"How about because I love her and I'm going to tell her it's always been real for me," Cody shoots back and all I can think about is he loves me. Cody loves me!!!

"Love," the Mayor sneers. "Do you really think love will keep you happy for the rest of your lives? Do you really think love earns you the right to marry my daughter?" Hold up. What?

"That's rich seeing as you've been hidden in the shadows her whole fucking life," Cody shoots back.

"Oh, and you think she's going to keep on loving you when she finds out you knew the deep dark family secrets the whole fucking time. Stay away from her. Let her go back to New York and stay there where she belongs," he thunders. I hear footsteps but I am too stunned to move. The door swings open and there is the Mayor in the door way, behind him is a shell shocked Cody.

"Angel, it's not what you think.," he says walking towards me.

"Stop," I shout. "Is it true?" I asked them, lowering my voice to just above a whisper.

"Yes," Cody says softly. "But I wanted to tell you."

"That doesn't matter!" I scream. "You lied."

"I didn't lie. I just didn't tell you."

"A lie of omission is still a lie," I say firmly.

"I told him not to tell you," the Mayor tells me.

"Was I just not good enough?" I ask him before holding up a hand. "Wait. I don't want to know. As far as I'm concerned. You're getting your wish. I'm going home and I never want to hear from either of you again. I will not ever beg for the affections of any man be it my lover or my father," I shrug off their excuses and wasted breaths.

"Angel," But I was already gone. I'd turned on my heel and was walking as purposefully as I could with my head held high. I almost didn't flinch when I heard Cody scream out one last time. "Angel!!" But like I said, I was already gone.

Cody

Nothing matters any more. Everything is…blank. Or at least, that's what I'm telling myself. Really, everything hurts. I thought Kimmy ripped my heart out. I was wrong. So fucking wrong. I didn't know what it was like to have and to love a good woman. And then I did. And then I subsequently lost said good woman and my life turned to shit. Not really. Everything is still the same. I'm still the head football coach for Tall Pines High School. I'm still the son and grandson of some amazing people. I still have friends in this town. Although some, like Sam, are defecting to Angel's side. And I can't blame them. I wish I was there too.

But I'm here. Sitting on the floor of my living room because the couch was too good for the likes of me. Actually, I got home from work; saw the couch and all I could think about was tickling Angel on the couch. Fucking Angel over the arm of the couch. So I grabbed a bottle of scotch, and sat on the floor. The floor is my friend, it doesn't judge me.

I also no longer sleep. I kind of just battle nap in between bouts of anger at everyone who told me to lie and self-loathing over how I could be such a moron. I just go back and forth back and forth. Never coming to a resolution.

Then in the mornings, I get up feeling like shit. And smelling of booze. So I tie on my running shoes and add some more punishment to my life. I run harder and farther. I work out longer when I get home. It is the only thing I have that even remotely takes some of the ache in my heart away. Not completely. Never completely. But if a little is all I can get. I'll take it. That's where I am. Those are my days. Lather, rinse, mother fucking repeat. It has been three days.

There's a knock on my door and I answer it with a scowl on my face. I totally don't care. There is absolutely no one I want to see with the exception of Angel, and I'm pretty sure she wishes I were dead. I am not surprised to see my scowl met by two scarier scowls. From my best friends, Sam and Holt; Who are holding brown paper bags and pizza.

"We came to tell you we're here to watch the game," Sam says.

"But really we're here to get you drunk and talk some sense into you," Holt finishes.

"Go away," I tell them.

"No," they say in tandem. I sigh and move away from the door, granting them entrance.

They head right to the coffee table and put the pizza boxes right on top. Holt, the more responsible of the two, goes to the kitchen and grabs the roll of paper towels and the bottle opener that magnets to my fridge.

I take the beer that's handed to me and sit back and wait for their intervention of my life. Sam leans back in his seat like he's king of his domain. Holt leans forward with his wrists resting on his knees. Here we go.

I knew we'd get here eventually. I just didn't think these two would bring out the big guns so early in the game. They aren't messing around. But I knew, sooner or later, we would arrive at this destination.

Right after Angel left my office, I lost it. I mean I mother fucking *street car named desire* all up in this place except instead of *Stella*, I screamed Angel over and over again. I screamed her name and tried to go after her, but her fucking father stopped me. He held me back and wouldn't let me go, whispering things that were fucking with my already fucked head. Things like, Let her go. and *You're not good enough for her* and my personal favorite, Look what you've done to her.

I was still screaming when Sam and my dad came running down the hall, hell bent for leather, only to find I had lost my ever-loving mind. I screamed and raged some more. The new arrivals still didn't know what was happening, but they soon figured it out.

When I realized everything I had lost, I gave up. I slump down the wall and buried my head in my hands. She's gone. That's all I could keep thinking. She's gone. She didn't let me explain. Wouldn't listen. After everything, she just walked away. Because in the end, they all walk away.

Sam and my dad were screaming at me to tell them what happened. I couldn't answer. I just sat there wallowing...like a girl... with Mayor McDoucheypants scowling at me from his place in the corner. Asshole.

Eventually, my dad told me in the nicest, manliest way possible to get my happy ass up or he was calling in the friendly guys with the funny white jackets and the butterfly nets. For fear of what would happen after they shot me with a tranquilizer gun, I got my happy ass up, grabbed my keys and headed home. I walked Steve up to my mom's and told him to stay with her.

Then I went home and got as drunk as I could, hoping against hope that the pain in my chest would fade. News flash: It didn't.

"So what are you going to do?" Sam asks me. I look up realizing I had zoned out for a while. Whoops.

"About?" I ask. Holt just shakes his head mumbling something about someone having shit for brains.

"Angie. Obviously," Sam snaps.

"What about Angie?" I ask.

"What about Angie? *What about Angie?*" He asks. Sam gripes.

"Do you love her?" Holt asks me, oddly quiet.

"Of course," I answered, meeting his eyes.

"Then go get her," he growls.

"You didn't see her. She doesn't want me. I hurt her," I tell them.

"You fucked up for sure. And dollars to donuts, you'll do it again. You have a dick; it's bound to happen. But bottom line, if you love her go get her," Holt says softly.

"He's right man," Sam tells me. "Look at Katy. She had the world in her hand and lost it at eighteen. Is that what you want? You want to walk around this town with a cloud over your head and everyone knowing you loved and you lost? That all that's left for you is death so you can join the one you love on the other side? Or are you going to fight? Don't you think if Katy could go back and change one thing so he came home from that tour, tell Will she loved him one more time, she would?"

"I never told her that I love her," I say choking back the less than manly tears.

"Buddy, she's wearing your grandmother's ring," Sam says to me. "If that isn't love, I don't know what is."

"Maybe you should tell her now," Holt tells me. But I just nod. I have to get my shit together for my Hall of Fame induction. Maybe after that, I'll find her and tell her how much I love her. How sorry I am when we've all had time to cool down.

"Okay. I'll think about it," I tell them. "So, what does it feel like to be the coach of the Under 6 league soccer champs this season?" I ask Sam.

"Damn good," He tells me on a soft smile. "Tomorrow morning is our last game of the season. It's going to be awesome!"

"I can't wait to hear all about it," I laugh as I tell him. But I never would. That morning, Sam and his daughters were on their way to their soccer game, the last game of the season when they were hit by a drunk driver and killed instantly. I can't help but think about Aliza now and Sam's own words of living life while you can, because in the end life is too damn short. And I miss my friend.

SIXTEEN

Angellica

I can't stop crying. This is ridiculous. I think my body actu-ally ran out of tears hours ago, maybe days, but my body is still sobbing. This morning, I cried so hard when I woke up that I threw up all over my bathroom. So then I spent the next hour sobbing and scrubbing like I'm Cinder-freaking-ella. It's a charming quality.

My head is pounding from crying for so long. My voice is hoarse, but I don't care. I know I should get up and take some aspirin, drink a bottle of water or twelve, and move on with my life. But I just can't.

I'm lying in my bed facing the door when I hear a knock. I don't want to talk to anyone, so I roll over and face the wall instead. If I'm really quiet they'll go away. I hope. But like always, my luck is absolute shit. I hear the knob turn and the door push open. I hold my breath and close my eyes. Soft steps cross the plush carpet of my bedroom. The bed gently depresses next to my back just a little.

"Baby girl, it's me," Aunt Mable whispers. I can hear the tears clogging her throat. She brushes her hand over my hair like she did when I was little, and I feel the hot tears roll down my cheeks. I guess I had some more in me after all. "I have something I have to tell you."

"No," I shake my head because I just can't handle it right now. "No. I'll be ok," I tell her.

"No, baby. Listen," she implores me. "When we were young, your mother and I. We grew up here in Tall Pines."

"I already know this stuff, Aunt Mable," I tell her sweetly.

"Hush, I'm tempted to swat your behind for interrupting, this is hard enough," she tells me.

"Okay. I'm sorry. I'll listen," I tell her.

"When we were growing up, Mayor Hart was just George, and he was mine. He wasn't the cold, hard man you see today. He was sweet and kind and he loved me very much. He wanted to run away and get married, but I wanted to wait. We were both in college. He was studying political science and I was studying nursing.

"His dad, the then Senator, felt he needed to learn a lesson. And my sister, your mother, was never one to shy away from opportunity, she went to the same party he was at one night. His father had just told him that if he married me, he would disown him, take his trust fund, and have him kicked out of school. The Senator liked everyone right where he wanted them to be, doing what he told them to.

"At this party George was licking his wounds deep in a bottle of whiskey. When Renee walked up to him, he thought she was me. We looked close enough alike that deep in the throws of intoxication, he wouldn't have known. I know that now. Anyway, she talked to him. He told her all about what happened, and she told him she would never leave him, no matter what. And then she suggested they go back to his apartment…. and well, it's your parents, so yeah. I think you can figure out that was about nine months before you were born.

"When George woke up he was terrified. He knew he had made a horrible mistake. He was furious. He yelled at her and Renee just laughed. She said she would tell me and he would never see me again. But it was worse than that. I saw them." My breath hitches in my chest. I know how bad that feels. Watching Joe and Erin. But it's nothing compared to losing Cody.

"I walked into the apartment looking for George and found him in bed with my sister. So I ran. I wouldn't listen, and I didn't care. I moved to New York and became a nurse. I mostly raised you because Renee was a total shit. I know it's not nice to speak ill of the dead, but still," she shrugs. It's the truth, so what can she do?

"But where do I come in? How come he didn't want me?" I ask.

"Oh, I forgot. A couple weeks later, Renee found out she was expecting and she and the Senator demanded George marry her and fall into the family fold again. But he said no. He would never marry her because of her part in things. He owned his role in it all, it was a mistake, but hers, was cruel. So he sent her packing. Said he would do everything else his dad wanted but marry, if he couldn't have me.

"Renee had no choice but to come to me and beg for help with the baby. She wasn't going to raise you on her own. George knew she would. He figured by giving you up, you would end up in my care and far, far away from the Senator. He felt it was the best he could do by you. But you have to know, he's looked out for you your whole life. He's the one who set up this opportunity for you after the fall out in New York."

I was reeling. I cannot believe the words, the picture Mable painted. How sad to be so unwanted, and yet so loved all at the same time. Mable, I guess did the best she could with a crappy situation, when she was very young. I guess I can relate, I did pretty much the same thing. And Cody didn't sleep with my sister. I've actually never been so glad that I don't have a sister before now.

"I see you're thinking things through. Moving forward, we can go in any direction you want to go, love. But now, we have to do something important."

"What's that Aunt Mable?" I ask.

"Baby, Saturday morning, Sam and the girls were killed in a car crash. Drunk driver. We have to go call on Aliza."

"Oh, no," I gasp. Poor Aliza. And poor Holt...And Cody.

"Yes, baby. So while you're thinking about the relationships in your life and who you want to keep and who you don't, maybe remember that life is short, and that some of us make bad mistakes with the best of intentions," she takes a deep breath. "And also, that I'll love you forever."

"I love you too. Let me clean up real quick and we can go see Aliza.

When we knock on the front door, a beautiful woman with long black hair answers. She looks sad, but thoughtfully, towards the stairs. I'm assuming this is where Aliza is living out her grief.

"We're here to see Aliza," Mable says.

"I'm Hannah, I'll tell her you called, but she's not really up to it right now," the woman tells us.

"Okay, we'll come back later," I said. "My aunt made these maple blondie squares," I try to hand the package off to Hannah.

"Hannah, was that the door?" Aliza asks. "Oh, hello Mable, Angie. Come on in," she tells us. We follow her into the living room where we all take a seat, where Hannah places the tin of blondies on the coffee table.

"I'll just go make some coffee," Hannah says to everyone and no one.

"Thank you," Aliza looks at her softly. Before looking directly at me. Her eyes staring into mine. It's unnerving.

"I'm sorry for your loss," I tell her. Instantly feeling like a chump for saying it because there are no way that those words can ever be enough.

"Thank you," she says before taking a deep breath, shoring up her courage. "Sam was the great love of my life. It kills me that he and the kids are gone. It kills me. But I would do it all over again in a heartbeat because they were the very best parts of me. Do you understand?" She asks of me, her eyes locked on mine.

"No," I shake my head.

"Don't throw away your happiness out of hurt and anger. Sam did so many stupid things. God, he could make me crazy. But, I loved him so much. And he loved me. Don't lose that."

"Okay," I say stunned.

"The funeral will be Tuesday at eleven o'clock. Anyway, I'm tired," she says politely as she stands.

"We should be going," Mable says. Oh, now she chimes in. Thanks for letting me hop on the train to crazy town with a grieving widow. Or was it really crazy? Could she be right?

Tuesday rolls around before anyone in this town is ready. I quietly dress in a simple black dress with cap sleeves and a tastefully rounded neckline. I open my jewelry box and Cody's ring winks at me. How I wish I could put it on with confidence and claim him as mine. But how can I believe any of it was true? How can I not?

I meet Mable downstairs and we head to the church without words. Today is not a happy day. The church is tall and white and beautiful, and filled with the whole town. Sam was not only a local hero returned home, but also a beloved football coach.

The service is sweet and sad and full of love. Sam's life was so full of love and nothing was more prominent than the love he had for his family. His friends and family spoke often of how Aliza and the girls were his world. The service is wrapped up in a slideshow of photos from his life to Old Dominion's *Til It's Over*. Pictures of Sam in his uniform, overseas, playing football, marrying Aliza, the birth of the girls and so on swirl through the music and beautiful words of loving while you can. It freezes on a picture of Sam and Aliza with their arms wrapped around each other and the girls. Everyone is smiling at the camera except for Sam who is looking at Aliza with all the love in the world in his eyes.

I see Cody as we all shuffle out of the church like cattle. He has been tasked as a pallbearer for one of the girls. Those who served with Sam, including Holt, are in their uniforms as they escort Sam's flag draped coffin. Cody looks devastated. When our eyes meet, he nods once before looking away. I see the Mayor, my dad, and he does the same. I know what I have to do, but this isn't the time or place.

SEVENTEEN

Angelica

My palms are sweating as I weave my way through all of the people in the stadium for Cody's Hall of Fame induction. Well, sweating is a term we should use loosely. My hands are like fire hoses gushing with sweat because I am so fucking nervous. Who in the world thought it would be a good idea to declare my undying love for a retired NFL player at his own induction ceremony? In front of millions? Shit, I'm going to have to change my identity when Cody shoots me down. I'll have to go incognito. Do you think I'll look okay as a brunette? Maybe a redhead? Oh, fuck. Who am I kidding? There is no possible way to conceal this ass.

I'm on the field with all of the press and the who's who of the professional football world. I look up, the stands are packed with fans. My heart beats a little faster because this is all for Cody and I want him to have everything possible in life. He already has my heart; Even if he doesn't want it.

I push my palms flat on my belly hoping to stop the *Cirque du Solie* act that's swinging around in my gut. My head is pounding. And I have to pee. I look up from my hiding spot behind some guy who obviously moonlights as a mountain range and see Holt taking the stage. Jim told me the order of speakers when he slipped me my pass and we cooked up this little scheme to humiliate me and my whole family for the rest of my life. I know I have time so I duck into the restroom.

I quickly do my business, which seems to happen more and more frequently these days. I should really have that looked at. I will. I swear. When I get home. Mark was right when he said Nurses make the worst patients. I have no desire to spend my free time in a hospital. Give me some Motrin and call it good.

I place my purse on the counter and turn the taps on to wash my hands. I wet a little paper towel and try to blot some of the sweat from my forehead, then my upper lip, and my pits. This shit is getting out of hand. I'm waving more paper towels around trying to create a breeze to dry my over active sweat glands when the door pushes open and I am greeted with the snarl of a face I will never forget.

"Well well. Look what the cat dragged in?" Kimmy says to the two groupies that followed her in. Her over inflated boobies are bobbing around in a dress with way too many sequins for a daytime event.

"Look how sweet her little pink dress is?" One of the crew mock coos. Honestly, I could give two shits. But they caught me doing my dying bird mating dance to clean up the shit show my nerves are causing on my look.

"Do I know you?" I ask as I pull my compact out of my purse and begin to powder my nose.

"Does she know us?" Kimmy asks and then answers her own question. "I know you know who I am. I remember you from the hospital, that night... so long ago."

"That was some fun times," I say off handed. I grab my lip gloss and swipe some on.

"And I see you've done pretty well for yourself; Filling in my rightful place at Cody's side these last few months, but all that is about to end," she tells me.

"Huh?" I ask. Because honestly, I have no idea.

"Come now," she laughs and her flying monkeys chime in. "You had to know it wouldn't last. He would always come back to me. I just can't wait to get my ring back and buy a new house here in New York," she babbles.

"New York? What about Texas?" I ask. Cody would never want to leave Tall Pines.

"I'm not living in that shit hole," she states.

"Well, I for one, like that shit hole," I say ramping up my mad. I'm pretty sure Kimmy went off the deep end a while ago, but still. I'm mad. "What about his team?" I ask.

"What about them?" Kimmy asks back.

"You're crazy, aren't you?" I ask. "Cody has no idea you're here."

"Really?" She purrs back. "Because last night we agreed to go to dinner," she says. And it could happen, but this feels off. Still, my hands are starting to sweat again. I wonder if this is how Carrie felt at the Prom.

"I don't believe you," I tell them.

"Who cares what you want because I want him back and nothing, and I mean nothing is going to stand in my way. Do you hear me little girl?" She snaps. "Because who would want a fat ass like you when they could have this perfection?" She asks with a sweeping gesture up and down her skinny body and inflated boobs. But the damage was done.

"Eeeaaarrrppp," I fling a hand over my mouth. I shake my head back and forth furiously to try and convey the back the fuck off message. Shit's going down. Mayday!!!! But Kimmy, dumb fuck that she is, just stands there staring at me with her head tipped to the side in the universal sign of what was that?

"What?" She steps closer. Oh no. I tried to warn her. "Whatever. Like you're a threat to me," she snaps. I open my mouth to tell her to back the fuck off forgetting the situation for a moment, when I pour the contents of my stomach all over Kimmy's ugly ass dress.

"Oh, gross," the other two girls scream.

"You fucking cow!" Kimmy shouts. "Look what you've done!"

"Well, this has been fun, but I think my work here is done. I'll see you around, girlfriends," I smile and wave. Don't let the door hit you on the way out.

I quickly make my way back through the crowds and hear Jim wrapping up his speech to Cody. So much love in that family. I love them all so much. He makes me think of my own dad. We have a long row to hoe to fix that mess, but I'm fairly sure we want to, most days. I even think he's in the crowd somewhere cheering me on. Or at least I hope so. Cody is it for me and I won't let anyone stand in my way.

I peek around the last row of press and see him standing there at the podium. God, Cody is handsome. I smile softly as I watch him. I could stare at this man for hours. The way he stands, the way he moves, the way he treats people. The way he always made me feel cherished and loved. I love this man. His eye catches mine and for the first time in a longtime, I see him smile. And I know it has to match my own.

EIGHTEEN

Cody

Wrong. That's how this whole thing feels. Just wrong. My suit is itchy. My tie is too tight. My heart hurts too much. Just. Wrong.

I'm sitting on the stage in New York awaiting my Hall of Fame induction. This should be the best day of my life. The culmination of everything I have ever worked for. And it is. But it's also not. My parents are sitting on the opposite end of the stage from me with proud smiles on their faces and heartache in their eyes. It's probably the way my face would look right now if I were able to smile. But that ship sailed when my girl wouldn't talk to me, and my best friend died.

Sam was supposed to be here with me. He's one of my coaches at the school, but before that we played on the same teams growing up; from peewee to college. There is no one else that knows me better. But last week, a drunk driver cut Sam's life short with one shitty decision. Not only that, but the lives of his daughters too. The last time I saw Sam, he was telling me to fix what was broken between Angel and I before it was too late. The irony is not lost on me.

The last time I talked to Angel, when it was good, before it went bad, she promised she would be here with me today. But she hates me, so she's not. I fucked it all up. I saw her at the funeral. She looked bad. Still devastatingly beautiful, but broken hearted, nonetheless. Gorgeous in her funeral dress, her wild blonde hair tastefully swept back and basic black heels. But her eyes. Her eyes were red rimmed and sad. I wanted to go to her. I barely held back knowing she wouldn't want that. And I had a duty to my friend. There are no words to describe being a pall bearer for your best friend's daughter. They split us up civilian friends and family escorted the girls, Marines escorted Sam's flag covered coffin. If I never do it again, it'll be too soon. I'll never forget the look on Holt's face as he presented the flag to Aliza. I rub my chest over the ache when the memory passes across my brain.

I kept thinking Angel would come to me, but she didn't. So after all was said and done and rifles fired, I hopped on a plane and headed east. I didn't intend to stay here long; just long enough to fulfill my media obligation, see my number retired, and my plaque added to the facility.

The interviews leading up to today's ceremony just about killed me. They kept asking about Sam, and how hard it must be for me to be here without him. Then they asked me about the woman I was rumored to be engaged to, and where she was presently. I was honest about the former and vague about the latter which was frustrating for all.

Holt, who is also here with us today, takes to the podium. He's supposed to introduce some photomontage of my life and career; everything that leads up to this moment. I have no idea what is in it. My family put it together and I'm nervous, but excited to reminisce with them.

"Good afternoon everyone, my name is Holden Stone, but don't call me that. Everyone calls me Holt. I've known Cody my whole life. In fact, Cody, my brother, and I were all born the same week.

"We spent our childhood together, with my twin brother, Will, and our dear friend, Sam, who we lost this week, but I know is looking down on us right now. We went fishing, camping, and played football like boys do. Cody was always ahead of the pack. But it wasn't just talent, he wanted it. He worked for it. When Cody and Sam got recruited to college, no one was surprised. Signing day and draft day were some of the best days of his life."Last night, I thought about what Sam and Will would want to tell you if they could be here today. And I think they would tell you that they're most proud of your drive and tenacity. You never gave up. Well, Sam, would feel like you need another pep talk on the subject but we'll talk about that later. But you did it. No matter how great the task, be it making the pros, making the super bowl, relearning how to walk, coaching the best team our town has had since you played to the state championships. You never gave up. So, without further ado, here is a look at the making of you, Cody."

Rascal Flatt's "Stand" plays over the loud speakers at the stadium while pictures of my life flash before me. A baby in a Dallas Cowboys outfit, a little boy running with a football that's as big as he is, my high school and college ball, that picture of me catching the ball before my career ending hit, then the newspaper clipping covering the accident and the end of my career, pictures of me in rehab in a wheelchair, then walking, coaching the War Eagles from the sidelines with Sam. Pictures of me with my family and friends interwoven. I'm momentarily surprised when a picture of Angel in my arms laughing slips by. The last picture is a picture of my kids celebrating a State Championship win on the field with me this last season. It freezes there until the song ends while my dad steps up to the podium and addresses me directly over the mic.

"Cody, my boy, my son, all grown up. You're mother told me to get up here and say a bunch of girlie shit about feelings, but that's not my style. And the only words I have for you is how very proud we are of you. You have never, not once, let us down. And I can't wait to see what the future has in store for you," he finishes cryptically before introducing me. "Without further ado, ladies and gentlemen, my son, Cody Reynolds."

I step up to the podium and give a great big hug to my dad, quietly thanking him for everything he has ever done for me, to encourage me, to inspire me my whole life, but for our ears only. When he resumes his seat, I take a deep breath and stick my fingers in my suit pockets; a nervous habit from way back.

I rock back on my heels, preparing for what I'm about to say, when I look up and see the face of an angel. Well, mine at least, is standing behind the last of the press seats, looking at me with nervous, wide eyes. God, I've miss those blue eyes. And suddenly, for the first time in days, I feel a smile on my face.

"I screwed up, baby," I say into the mic. Angel's face goes beat red. "You deserved the truth, no matter how hard. I wanted to protect you and I failed. Tell me you forgive me."

She just nods. The wave of press looks to her and then back to me.

"Okay, now tell me you love me."

The press laughs and looks to her again. And again she nods.

"Okay, last question, tell me you'll marry me," I ask her and then hold my breath.

The press swings back to her in full tennis match fashion. And again, she nods.

"Seriously?" I ask. Getting excited.

"Yeah, baby," she beams at me.

"Come here, baby," I tell her, holding out my hand and she does not disappoint when she does not hesitate to make her way to me. When she reaches me, she wraps her arms around my middle and buries her face in my chest.

"I love you, baby," I tell her. "I'm going to make you so happy." She looks up at me, and smiles, but something flashes in her eyes. And then she hurls all over me like she's the first President Bush and I'm a Japanese dignitary, then promptly passes out in my arms. Yep, that's totally ending up on YouTube later.

"We're going to need a medic," I call out.

The ride to the Emergency Room was not as short as it would have been in Tall Pines, but short for New York. It is not lost on me, as I sit in the bay with Angel next to the hospital bed she's laying in while we wait for her lab results, that this is the hospital where I first saw her after my accident; convinced she was an angel -- and she is -- but now she's mine. This time our combined family and friends who were in town for the ceremony, sit in the waiting room, worried for Angel.

"Hey Marie," she says when an older nurse comes through the curtain. "What's up?" She asks and then the doctor that saw her when we came in is behind her.

"I wanted to be here for the goods," she says cryptically.

"Fred?" Angel asks the older doctor, who smiles kindly at her.

"I know why you're sick and I know why you passed out," he tells her.

"Okay. Well, hit me with some Tamiflu and send me back to Texas," she snaps.

"You're pregnant, Angie." And there is a roaring in my ears. I couldn't have heard him correctly. Thankfully, Angel asks him to repeat himself.

"WHAT?!" She hollers.

"Angie, you're pregnant. Congratulations!"

"Mable is going to be fit to be tied when she finds out I knew first!" Marie cackles. I throw my head back and laugh. Poor Angel looks shell-shocked. That is until she hears me laugh.

"What are you laughing at?" She snaps.

"We'll just leave you alone for now while we go get the ultrasound machine. Be right back."

"You, this baby, everything. It's everything I ever wanted," I look at her. "And we're getting married, like yesterday. I'll fly us right to Vegas, or I'll give you until September to throw a wedding together, which is plenty of time if you factor in Mable, my mother, and grandmothers. But that's it. I won't wait a day longer," I smile at her.

"You're ok with this?" She asks me.

"Of course," I tell her. "You want a boy or a girl?" I ask.

"I'm happy either way," she says softly. As the nurse and doctor wheel in this funny looking computer and plug it in.

The doctor starts tapping away at the keys and a weird yellow wave appears on the screen. This must be what we were waiting for. Then the doctor puts a giant stick in some interesting places and before I can comment, the most beautiful sound in the world surrounds us. It's strong and rapid like drums in a marching band.

"Strong heartbeat," the doctor says.

"That's the heartbeat?" I ask, staring at the screen. The doctor punches some more keys and something flutters over the screen. And then I see it. It's a baby. It's my baby. "Holy shit," I say, Angel's hand clutched in mine.

"That's our baby," she says softly.

"That's our everything," I say before leaning over her to brush the hair off her face. Planting a grateful kiss on her temple. Angel and the baby, *that's my everything.*
You Should Be Here

EPILOGUE

Aliza

My Dearest Sam,

     Today, I'm standing on the most beautiful beach. Remember how we said we'd take a second honeymoon down to the Keys some day? Well, I'm here, baby. But I can't help thinking you should be here. I can't help wondering why you left me? Why did you take the girls with you? How could you leave me behind, Sam? How can I possibly go on now? But these aren't questions for today.

     Today is Angie and Cody's wedding. You were right, baby, they figured it out. So here we are on the beach. I'm wearing a lovely, short silk dress that blows in the breeze. Holt said it's the perfect color gray to make my eyes pop. He calls them my wild Irish eyes. Says they're so green that I must have been blessed by the fairies as a babe. Holt says a lot of things like that. I don't know how to feel about that, Sam. He makes me feel beautiful and special. And I love it. But he also makes me feel like I'm cheating. Like I broke my vows to you, Sam. Or I'm about to. I wish you were here to tell me what to do. You always gave the best advice. Maybe send me a sign?

     Did you know, he walked me down the aisle? Holt did. He is one of Cody's groomsmen, I'm a bridesmaid. He walked me slowly, like he was born to do it with my arm in his and my bouquet in my other hand. At the end, when we reached the alter made of willow and driftwood, he leaned down and kissed the top of my head. It was so sweet. So in the moment.

Now I'm standing here watching Angel and Cody exchange their vows. They wrote their own. Remember ours? You pledged to be my protector and champion and to put the toilet seat down for all times. And I? I promised to love you and be your home no matter where the Marine Corps sent us and to never complain about how bad your PT gear smelled because smelly PT gear is a blessing, it means you came home to me. I still can't believe after all those missions, all the hush hush super secret squirrel crap in God forsaken places, it was a stupid soccer game you didn't come home from. I'm still a little angry, Sam. At you. At God. At everyone who gets to go on living their life while I'm stuck in limbo waiting.

I made it through their vows, babe. Just one little tear burned down my cheek. I couldn't hold it back. But I did it with a smile on my face. I know it's not quite real, but I'm trying. I'm trying so damn hard today, Sam. Holt saw it. He looks sad when he looks at me. It hurts me to know I'm making him sad, but I don't know how to stop. My hurt is so much greater. My emotions so much more conflicted.

There they are now, man and wife. Such a beautiful place to be.

With the ceremony complete, Cody and Angel seal their vows with a kiss. A very hot kiss. You would have whooped louder than anyone at their display. Laughing. I can almost feel your arms around me. I look up and catch Holt's eye. He looks angry. No. Determined. Holt looks determined about something. And he's looking at me. I feel a sizzle in my belly and wariness in my chest. What do you think your dear friend is up to, my love? Just send me a sign, baby. Tell me what to do. Please. Until then, I'll be here waiting. Until we meet again.

All my love, until my last breath,
Aliza

The End...For Now

Stay tuned for an excerpt from Aliza's story,
Whiskey Lullaby.

My House – Flo Rida

Mayday – Cam

Crazy Sexy Beautiful – Old Dominion

T-Shirt – Thomas Rhett

Til It's Over – Old Dominion

Stand – Rascal Flatts

Hall of Fame - the Script ft. will.i.am

You Should Be Here – Cole Swindell

AUTHOR'S NOTE

If you enjoyed this story, and I sincerely hope you did, I am going to let you in on a little secret. My grandfather was an amazing man. He was brilliant, had a dry sense of humor that was funny in itself, and was so full of love and laughter everyone around him felt it. My grandfather also had the soul of a storyteller. In fact he wrote a book. But before his novel had made it through the editing stages, he was living with a new reality. One that he did not choose but was chosen for him. For years, we watched him struggle with the effects of the disease. Alzheimer's took my brilliant, sweet grandfather from us long before the disease claimed his body from this earth. And to this day, his book is still unpublished.

You might ask yourself, why would I share this with you? And the answer is easy. In real life, I am shy. I never thought I would put any of my stories out there for anyone other than myself or my husband to see. Until last year, when my grandfather passed, and I thought about his unfulfilled dream. And through it, I realized a dream of my own and also, maybe, a little piece of his storyteller's soul in me. So while these are my words, not his, the publishing of this piece and the others that will follow are that realization. So, this is for you, for me, but mostly for my grandpa. Thank you for helping us achieve that dream.

Also, if you or someone you love is living with Alzheimer's disease, know that you're not alone. My family and I pray that one day there will be a cure. But until then, you are in our thoughts and hearts. And if this disease has not played a direct part in your life, but our story has and you feel moved, you can find ways to donate, walk, or volunteer at www.alz.org.

XOXO,
Jennifer

ABOUT THE AUTHOR

Jennifer is a 32 year old lover of words, all words: the written, the spoken, the sung (*even poorly*), the sweet, the funny, and even the four letter variety. She is a native of San Diego, California where she grew up reading the Brownings and Rebecca with her mother and Clifford and the Dog who Glowed in the Dark with her dad, much to her mother's dismay.

Jennifer is a graduate of California State University San Marcos where she studied Criminology and Justice Studies. She is also a member of Alpha Xi Delta.

10 years ago, she was swept off her feet by her very own sailor. Today, they are happily married and the parents of a 7 year old and 6 year old twins. She can often be found on the soccer fields, drawing with her children, or reading. Jennifer is convinced that if she puts her fitbit on one of the dogs, she might finally make her step goals. She loves a great romance, an alpha hero, and lots and lots of laughter.

This is her debut novel.

You can connect with Jennifer at:

JenniferRebeccaAuthor.com

E-mail: JenniferRebeccaAuthor@gmail.com

Facebook: facebook.com/JenniferRebeccaAuthor

Twitter: @JenniRLreads

Instagram: JenniRLreads

OTHER BOOKS BY
JENNIFER REBECCA

The Southern Heartbeats Series

Stand, Vol 1
Whiskey Lullabye, Vol. 2 *(Coming Soon)*
Just A Dream, Vol. 3 *(Coming Soon)*

The Funerals and Obituaries Mysteries

Dead and Buried, Book 1 *(Coming Soon)*

ACKNOWLEDGEMENTS

First and foremost, thank you. Thank you for reading this book. Thank you for following me on this journey. And thank you for giving me this opportunity to thank the people in my life that have made this moment possible.

Thank you to Alyssa Garcia at Uplifting Designs for creating the gorgeous cover and formatting. She is so talented and I cannot wait to see what she comes up with next.

Thank you to my awesome editor, Vicki Pierce, who also happens to be my mom. She graciously took time out of her busy schedule of being a grandmother to edit this book. But also for loving it and not just because she's my mom, but for the story that it is. Thank you for thinking this is cool and not that I lost my mind.

Thank you to my dad, Col. John Pierce, USMC Retired, for all of his military advice. He makes research easy and he has the best stories just waiting to be told. He is a great sounding board for plotlines and I love that. And also, because when I told him I was writing romance novels, his response was, "I'm not surprised."

Thank you to Alyssa Garcia and Stacy Garcia at GSBB, they are my OG Betas. This story was really written for them before anyone else ever saw it. They believed in me before anyone outside of my husband even knew I was writing and encouraged me to put myself out there. Not to mention, they are the best roommates on a girls' book weekend. Special thanks to Kellie for jumping on this crazy train to help me figure out what is good, but also what isn't. And for being one of the kindest people I have met on the book work journey.

Thank you to my dear, sweet, funny, and sometimes filthy Mixens. You all have welcomed me into the fold this year with kind hearts and open arms and there are not enough words to express how much I love and value these friendships. Thank you for answering my questions, for holding my hand, and also issuing a swift kick in the pants when I needed it. And also, you guys can rock a blurb like nobodies business. You guys are truly amazing.

Thank you to my husband, Sean, for everything. For celebrating harder than me when I was finally able to type the words "the end." For loving me. For always laughing when I say the phrase, "This still isn't the craziest thing I have done in ten years of marriage...." For supporting this dream whole-heartedly. For listening to my words. And for understanding how important this journey became September 2015.

Thank you to my children for being so awesome and so funny. I swear, we'll eat more creative meals than spaghetti this week...maybe. And also, may you never read this before age 30. I would hate to have to explain to the elementary school the new vocabulary you picked up from mommy's books.

Aliza

The warm, late spring sun is shining through the window when I wake up softly this morning. Sam is pressed up behind me. Close enough, I can tell he's feeling playful. He's left hand is at my breast and I feel his morning beard across my cheek as he leans down to kiss the side of my neck, just under my ear. I hear the soft smile in Sam's morning scratchy voice as he says, "Morning, baby," I love quiet moments like this.

"Good morning, handsome," I give back as Sam's hand trails over my belly. Softer than it was when we first met as teens, but it did carry his two babies, so he loves it, and moves down to greener pastures. I rock into him. Not once in the last fifteen years, have I gotten tired of him. Sam grabs my long brown ponytail tipping my head back so he can thoroughly kiss me. I love his kisses. The soft sweet ones, the teasing one, and the ones like this that get down to business. I moan into his mouth and Sam meets it with a growl of his own.

Things are just starting to get good when I hear two little voices chanting down the hallway, "Let's go Blazers. Let's go Blazers. Let's Goooooo!!!! The roof, the roof, the roof is on fire. We don't need no water let the mother effer burn!!!!" Sam's forehead is pressed down on my shoulder and his arms are wrapped tight around my belly. So tight, I can feel him shaking with laughter.

"Sam!" I screech when the shock of my precious angels chanting an inappropriate song from the 80's. I know exactly where they got it, that rat! I reach over to swat the stinker with a pillow from my side of the bed, but he's already moving. Throwing his shorts on the floor as he struts to the shower. Letting me see exactly what I will be missing today and I will be missing it. Damn, my man is good looking.

"What?!" Sam says on the run. "Soccer waits for no one!!!" He's laughing as he runs in the shower.

Twenty minutes later, my girls are pounding pancakes and bacon with tall glasses of orange juice. Fueling up for the big game. Six and under soccer is no joke. Sam walks in and I feel my breath catch in my throat. These are the moments I live for. My kids doing normal everyday things, the sexiest man I know, who after all this time, still looks at me like he won the lottery.

I catch Sam's secret smile as he walks over to the coffee pot and pours himself a cup. I catch a kiss on the cheek as he passes.

"I'm sure going to miss you guys today," I say and it's true. I never miss a game, but my best girlfriend from college is coming in today and I need to get to the market and prep dinner, put clean linens on the guest bed, and pick up any wayward toys that have made their way back out of the girls' rooms. Really, the things I need to do without a five and a three year old under foot.

"Don't even worry about it," Sam reassures me. "We'll be fine today, right girls?" Who throw their fists in the air with a "Heck, yeah!" Sam's influence and personality are all over those two. Sometimes, I think I was just the oven that baked the cake. "Plus, it'll be totally worth it at supper time when I get to dive in to your famous pot roast and green beans," he says while patting his stomach which is just as flat as it was at twenty when I got my first glimpse of him.

"Alright girls, you about done?" I ask them. "You don't want to be late for the big game." I smile at the three most important people in the world to me. This moment, like so many others, is why I breathe, why I wake up in the morning.

Sam gives me one more, soft kiss and the girls each hug me fiercely on their way out the door. Those three are going to have such a fun day.

I shut the door behind them and go back to the kitchen to clean up my mess from breakfast. I love to cook but I am not the cleanest cook either, but my family loves it. And is there really anything better than cooking for the people you love? Nope, I didn't think so. At least not to me.

After I have put the last of the dishes away, I clean up the girls' toys and pajamas they've left all over in their wake for soccer glory. I make the beds and wipe down the bathroom counters. I throw on jeans and my favorite slouchy sweater. I have just enough time to run to the market and get home before Hannah gets here when there is a knock at the door. I run down the stairs with a smile on my face. Sam is amazing, but he's a mess sometimes. Always forgetting something.

"What did you guys forget this time?" I shout as I throw open the door. But it's not Sam I see standing there. It's his best friend, Holt, and by the devastated look on his face, I know why. Everything changes in a moment.

Made in the USA
Columbia, SC
20 January 2018